SHADES OF
REALITY

LEIGH HAIG

INTRODUCTION BY
MICHAEL MCBRIDE

AFTERWORD BY
GENE O'NEILL

GALLOWS
PRESS

SHADES OF REALITY
© 2014 Leigh Haig
Trade Paperback Edition

ISBN-13: 978-0615880297
ISBN-10: 0615880290

Published by
GALLOWS PRESS 2014
Moosup, Ct. 06354

Cover, Interior Design, and Typesetting
© Tom Moran
Introduction © 2014 Michael McBride
Afterword © 2014 Gene O'Neill

Editing
Jamie La Chance , Billie Moran

www.gallowspress.com

Dedication

For Penny and Erin: it's a crazy world, and you let me do crazy things.

Acknowledgements

Being 'solo' published for the first time leaves me with too many to thank. For those not listed, my sincerest apologies. If I do this again, I'll try to catch you then.

Penny and Erin: you give me the time to pretend I can do more than just the day job.

Tom and Billie Moran: for giving an unknown a shot, lending plenty of enthusiasm and encouragement along with the acceptance, and for valuable suggestions with the story. And for everything in between that led to this completed book.

Mike McBride and Gene O'Neill: no words can convey the thanks for everything. From the encouragement, to mentioning my tale to Tom during an Internet chat to promote your own book. And of course adding your own words bookending mine. A pro should be so lucky to have that happen, let alone a hack.

Chris Hansen: you've made this much better than it ever would have been under my sole control...sorry I used up all of your red ink!

Paul Goblirsch: since the day I mentioned the sale of the story, your enthusiasm and excitement has not waned. You helped me maintain both of those for myself.

Steve Clark and Tasmaniac: thanks for my first ever story sale!

The publishers and authors I have worked with: you've given me a peek behind the curtain and kept my interest in publishing and writing active. Who knew this would happen?

And finally to those who are reading this: there are so many great writers out there whose book you could have bought instead of this one (like Mike and Gene, for example). I sincerely hope you feel satisfied with your decision when the last page is turned.

Introduction

The Stuff of Nightmares
By Michael McBride

There are very few things that genuinely scare me.

I haven't lost any sleep planning how I will handle the imminent zombie apocalypse, nor do I worry about brooding androgynous vampires romancing my teenage daughter. I seldom sweat transformation by wolf bite and figure the devil probably has better options than me when it comes to possession. But anything that could potentially threaten my children? That's a different story.

That's the stuff of nightmares.

As a parent, you're entrusted with the most precious and sacred of gifts. There's no greater responsibility. You have a fragile organism whose entire life is in your hands, the hands of someone far too human, someone who loses car keys and can't remember to put the seat down and sniffs the clothes in the hamper to see if they're clean enough to wear and will literally dive onto the floor to grab a dropped potato chip before the dog can beat him to it. It's a wonder any child survives long enough to procreate. It's hard enough to contend with the catastrophes over which you can exert some kind of control, and even then it's a tenuous kind of control at best.

And then there are the things that are outside of our control.

This is where true terror lives. If you're a parent, then you know exactly what I mean. Car accidents. Diseases. Warfare. A blink of an eye and it can all be over. Years of raising a child, loving a child, tending to every need and every whim and scrape and bruise and cavity...gone in a heartbeat. And even though you know that every time you send your child out the door you're running the risk that he or she might not walk back through it again, you play the odds and send them out into the world anyway, for you understand that you cannot swaddle them in bubble wrap and keep them in your sight at all times.

Worse still are the things for which there is no prevention. No cause. No rhyme or reason.

Alive one moment, dead the next.

And no one knows why.

This is where Leigh Haig takes us with his debut novella...to the fine line between life and death, where even an errant breath can tip the scales one way or the other. To say that this is a disturbing tale would be to do it a disservice. This is the kind of story that will stay with you long after you turn the last page.

It's obvious that Leigh is a father, for he captures the fear and the uncertainty, the disparate feelings of hope and the hopelessness, that any parent who has paced a darkened nursery in the middle of the night with a screaming child against his chest has undoubtedly felt countless times. The feeling of knowing that you would rip the still-beating heart out of your own chest with your bare hands if there was even the most remote chance that your sacrifice would guarantee your child's health.

This is a tale meant to explain the inexplicable, to bring order to chaos.

In short, ladies and gentlemen, you're wasting your time on these words when there is some intense reading ahead of you.

It's been my distinct pleasure to watch Leigh develop as an author. He's a class act, and one of the truly special people in the genre. At least I think so, anyway.

Of course, I could be wrong...I can't understand a bloody word he says.

Michael McBride
June 2011
Avalanche Country

Shades of Reality

Chapter 1

A sound pulls me from my sleep, interrupting a dream of vague powerlessness. I slowly slip back into the dream's tendrils when the sound comes again. Since Lucas came home from the hospital five months ago after his birth, every noise that has awoken me during the night has been from him, sleeping in the next room. But right now, my heart is hammering, my senses heightened as though my subconscious has detected a threat, not my crying son. Is there someone in the house? In the room? In *his* room?

I open my eyes to this thought and see the darkness of the room; no light seeps around the window furnishings, only the red glow from the clock gives any illumination. There isn't enough light to see anything in the room that shouldn't be here, no *deeper* darkness in the corners. I listen, my ears straining for any unusual noise, save for the light snoring from Jenny, my wife of fourteen years who is deeply asleep next to me, oblivious to what is happening.

I hear a whimper, a baby's cry. *Oh Jesus.* Relief washes over me. The thought of an intruder was very real; it had my entire body tense with worry, but it is only Lucas.

I lie in bed waiting to see if he will cry out again, if he'll need to be re-settled, hoping he won't. It's the tail-end of winter, and now that I am awake, I can feel the cool air of the house pressing against my exposed face, the rest of my body cocooned in in the warmth of the doona, where I want to stay.

Another cry—this one louder—signals that Lucas isn't going to put himself back to sleep. *Damnit.* I slowly climb from beneath the covers, the mattress groaning under the

movement, followed by a squeak from the bed's frame. My body, clad only in boxers, is engulfed by frigid air. My nipples stiffen; another part of me shrinks. As at all times like this, I regret the lack of central heating in the house, and recall fondly the previous house that was heated throughout the night. If only we hadn't decided we needed to buy a house and stop renting, before we started a family.

I glance over my shoulder to make sure Jen hasn't stirred. She's still snoring. Sliding my feet into my waiting slippers (the mental image of a blade slicing through my Achilles tendon, an image from my favourite movie, passes across my mind). I reach to the floor to grab my dressing gown. Technically it's not mine, since I've never bothered with one. But with it being winter and the chance I'll be getting out of bed in the early hours to an unheated house, I have been borrowing one of Jenny's, the manliest one she has: dark blue with white stars of varying sizes scattered across it. Wearing it I become Harry Potter, but without the wand or wizard friends.

I slip my arms into the gown as Lucas emits another cry, this one sounding a little more frantic. "It's alright little one, daddy's coming. Everything'll be fine," I whisper. I look over my right shoulder again, this time at the clock, its soft glow providing some illumination of Jenny's sleeping face. It's 3:58am, too early to stay up, so I make a date with my bed for, hopefully, a few short minutes from now, and head towards my little boy.

*   *   *

His room is not as cold as my own, the oil heater we leave on overnight doing the job of taking the crispness from the air. I stand just inside the doorway for a moment enjoying

the temperature change. Although we only have the heat turned low, it helps take the chills from my own body, not yet fully warmed by the dressing gown. I had read some time back that overheating in sleeping children was linked to cot death, the mysterious passing of a child in their sleep, so we were very cautious as to how warm we'd allow the room to be throughout the night. Having gone through what we did to finally have a child, I was prepared to suffer some cold nights to remove a potential risk to his wellbeing.

The cheap carpet crinkles under my feet as I walk to the cot. My eyes haven't adjusted to the dark, and I hold my right hand out, slowly moving it like a blind man's cane, as I edge ever closer to where the cot should be. My hand touches its cool wooden edge, giving me my bearings. Sliding up next to it, I squat down and reach between the wooden slats to give Lucas a reassuring rock, and whisper comforting words, to help send him back to sleep.

*　　　*　　　*

When Lucas is settled, I slowly rise to my feet, my left knee popping as I do so. I figure it's taken about ten minutes, which I'm pretty happy with. Wanting to be quiet and avoid disturbing the little one, I edge myself backwards and slip through the doorway, silently closing the door behind me.

As I turn, a shudder passes through my body, an icy cold finger trailing its way up my spine and out along both arms, causing goose bumps to prickle my skin. This is followed by an onslaught of light headedness and a flash of pure white light behind my eyes, the combined effect causing me to momentarily swoon. The earlier feelings of my dream rush back at me, and I have a vague sense of something being wrong. The spinning slows and then stops, almost as

sudden as it arrived.

"You're getting old," I mutter to myself giving a quick shake of my head, dislodging the uneasiness that had crept over me.

I turn to my room and raise my hand to push the door open, but it stands wide open. We normally leave it open during the night, but I am sure I pulled it closed on the way to Lucas so there would be less chance of any further cries waking Jen. *Yep, getting old*, I tell myself again, obviously having not closed the door.

Entering the room I check the clock. The numerals confuse me, showing 3:10. My mind flashes back to the clock when I left the room, I am sure it read 3:58. But that couldn't be; clocks don't run backwards for no reason. I stand stationary and puzzle this through my mind, finally hitting the logical conclusion that I had mistakenly read 2:58 as 3:58. The self doubt and hint of worry fade away.

With another shake of my head and inward berating of my foolishness, I walk towards the bed, removing the dressing gown.

Preparing to climb back into bed, I reach to pull the doona back but let out a yelp as my hand brushes a bare arm at the edge of the bed.

Chapter 2

I take a step back from the bed, a cloud of confusion floating across my mind, another cold finger of fear scraping down my spine. Jenny wears pyjamas to bed so I couldn't have felt her arm. Plus, even though the contact was brief, I'm sure I felt the light brush of hair against the tips of my fingers before jerking my hand away. Jenny keeps her arms silky smooth.

Composing myself and searching for a logical reason for the strangeness that seems to be surrounding me tonight, I look closely at my side of the bed, relying on the minimal light from the alarm clock. Darkness shrouds the bed, with nothing visible.

I then realise that I am still wearing my dressing gown, its soft fuzz a noticeable presence against my skin. This new strangeness atop those already swirling through my mind, forces my hand. I reach out to turn on my bedside light, but am halted by a scream.

Chapter 3

I drop my hand away from the light and turn towards Lucas's room, the source of the screaming, which has momentarily distracted me. His cry is frenzied, unlike normal. But I just came from his room, so I know his cry cannot be anything beyond some distress, of which I am feeling my own. I turn back to the bed—needing to first stem my own concerns and distress before returning to Lucas—when light floods the room. I raise my hand to shield against the brightness, but this is a reaction only, for the sudden illumination is not inflicting the pain normally felt when my eyes are assaulted with bright light from an almost total darkness.

My hand falls to my side and I turn to the source of the light. Lucas is still screaming, but I want to assure Jenny it's OK, that I'll go to him.

Jenny's bedside light is on, its glow causing the shadows of the room to slink into the corners, and hide behind the room's furniture. Lucas's cries still reverberate through the room, his pained wails piercing my heart more painfully than a knife could surely do. But I am rooted to the carpet, unable to go to him as much as I need to. For illuminated in the yellow glow are two forms in our bed. One, my beautiful Jenny, sitting up with her hand on the lamp, eyes blinking the harshness of the light away. The other, only now rousing but face visible, is myself, lying next to Jenny, eyes squeezed tight against the room's brightness.

Chapter 4

I cannot comprehend what I am seeing as my own form sits up in bed and turns to Jenny (do the eyes briefly stop on *me*?) who is climbing out of bed and reaching for her own dressing gown draped across the chair beside the bed. Confusion fights against the horror of what I am witnessing, an inability for my mind to process what it's being shown. I close my eyes tight, opening them again expecting the insanity of my vision to have normalised. The scene remains unchanged. Some*thing* that resembles me exactly, is lying in my bed.

I look to Jen, seeking some sign to halt the madness that's shrouding me. But I see nothing, no acknowledgement that I am even in the room.

"You stay here, dear, let me go to him," I hear the imposter saying, using my voice, and words I have uttered myself many times before. I continue to stare, a myriad of thoughts scrambling through my mind, a fear that I have gone insane and am imagining things. Lucas has momentarily gone silent, probably drawing breath ready to cry out again.

Jenny looks over at my doppelganger and gives him a weary smile. "I need to go to the loo anyway, Nigel. And he may be hungry since he didn't feed well before I put him down, so I may just put him on the breast and see. You stay warm." Then she yawns, stands and covers her slight frame with her robe.

The paralysis that I only now realise holds me motionless and silent, breaks. My hand reaches across the gulf of our bed towards my wife.

"Jenny? What's going on? Am I dreaming?" I cannot put words to the storm that blows through my mind, and feel like I am talking gibberish, surely another sign that my sanity has slipped away from me during the night. Something that cannot be happening *is* happening.

My words have no effect; there is no reaction from her, no indication she can even see me, which is ridiculous since I am bathed in light and she *must* have seen me when she turned to talk to the *other* me. The other me...

"If you want me to take over at all, just let me know." My voice once again, but not coming from me. My head swivels back to Jen as she shuts off the light, darkness racing to reclaim the room.

I hear her movement and I match it, wanting to cut her off and tell her how unfunny this is, for this must be some elaborate joke; it has to be, for any other alternative is unthinkable, unbearable. Yet for a joke, this is surely taking things too far; we both like a laugh at the others' expense, but this has become too much. I meet her at the corner of the bed, a vague shape in the darkness, slightly limned in red, and put my hand out to stop her movement. Since Lucas is still quiet, I want to end this crazy charade and allow the fear to drain from me and give me the chance to see the funny side.

Instead of stopping, Jen walks right through me. Not around me; not pushing me out of the way, but *through* me. I feel a blinding pain as she does so, like someone has thrown boiling water over my body, burning all nerve endings. I scream from the intensity and shock of the pain and also the blood curdling horror of what just happened. A realisation hits me, and hits me hard. I'm dead. But as fast as that thought comes, on its heels is the knowledge that it cannot be: if I am dead, how can I be in the bed and talking

LEIGH HAIG

to Jen? Has part of me died, the part that is standing in the middle of the room in confusion, whilst an element continues to live?

I shake my head, lost in a stupor. None of this makes sense. I need to keep moving, follow Jenny and see if I can find out what's going on. See what she knows. She has always been the stronger and smarter one, and I need her to use both of those assets now, for I am crumbling in fear, panic and confusion, the three swirling together to form a chaos within my body like I have never known. And there is a deep sense of loss. I am gone from my beautiful wife and child, and they are gone from me. It is this deep ache and realisation that finally gets me moving again.

Jenny has left our room so I follow her, noticing there is no sound of the carpet under my feet as I tread, not even the whisper of the dressing gown (that I shouldn't be wearing, for I had taken it off; I *know* that) as it moves against itself. I have walked the route from the bedroom into the nursery many times in the dead of night and never have I done so in complete silence.

Casting it aside, adding it to the rapidly expanding list of craziness that needs sorting, I exit our bedroom, feeling numb all over. Jenny has pulled Lucas's door closed and I can hear her quietly talking to him in her soothing motherly voice, soft cries his reply, and then a pale glow lightens the crack around the partially open door. The nightlight has been put on so she can put him on the breast. I reach out to push the door, but my hand passes *through* it, the door unmoved. This should shock me, but deep down I find I was almost expecting it, for I have a foreboding dread that I am no longer a part of the world that I have inhabited for over forty years.

I glide through the door (ignoring the impossibility of

20

SHADES OF REALITY

this, expected or not) and stop, staring at Jen as she nurses Lucas to her breast, dressing gown and pyjama top open just enough to allow it. The nightlight's glow is soft, romantic even, bathing them both in its blue hue. Although it does not pick out her facial features, it adds a glow to the blond hair framing her face. I imagine I can see the splattering of freckles that spread from eye to eye across the bridge of her nose. I can also hear (*and how is it that I can hear,* I wonder, *when I sure as shit don't exist*) the noise of Lucas's feeding.

Jenny is looking at the door, but staring off into the distance. With me now standing inside the room, if I *could* be seen, I would be clearly visible to her, whether she was looking into the distance or not. But there is no recognition, no sign that she sees me. I know it is futile before trying, but I try anyway; maybe my words will be heard even if I cannot be seen.

"Jen? Please help me Jen. I'm scared. Real scared. And real confused." I pause, not sure what else can be said. "Some weird shit's happening and you have to help me." The words float into the room. I can hear them, but they hold as much weight as my actual self, for Jenny doesn't register any sign of hearing me. I go to her and reach for her shoulder, but my fingers pass through it and I feel a fierce pain in them—the same pain as when she walked through me on her way to where she sits now. I move to place my hand on my son's head, but am rewarded with nothing different: incredible pain as my hand passes through his head as though it, or my hand, is made of nothing more than mist.

My son, who is more important than life itself and brings me joy every time I hold him, is lost to me. I know I should feel immense pain in my heart, but my body, or what I currently have as a body, seems incapable of the pain my real body knows all too well. Numbness is all it knows now.

I want to sit down against the wall and cry, but something occurs to me. I cannot feel my wife or child; I get nothing but pain for trying. But when I returned to bed after settling Lucas I felt an arm in my bed. No pain, just the flesh as my fingers brushed across it.

Turning to go and investigate this thought, I reach for the door handle, but of course my hand passes right through it. I return to my bedroom, and stop beside my side of the bed. Before I can ponder what I am going to do, I reach out a hand, intending to feel where I would expect the head to be if someone was lying there. I feel a slight tremble as my hand slowly extends, and lowers towards a head...or an empty pillow.

Just when I think the only thing I'll feel will be a pillow (normality having returned me from the *Twilight Zone*), my fingers brush against something fleshy with a little bit of yield and then press against something hard. I move my hand slightly up and the fingers brush against short, spiky hair: the way I wear mine. I jerk my hand away, not sure if I am happy with being able to feel this face, or more scared because of it.

"Don't do that." Whispered words float from the darkness. The voice is my own, but I didn't speak them. "Just leave me here for the night, and in the morning, or as soon as it is convenient, I will tell you what's going on."

Anger immediately rushes through me. "No." I am fuming, my voice raised to a near yell. "Tell me now or God help me I'll hurt you before you have the chance to move." I have no patience for this, and I'm shaking with rage now that I have something to vent at. I reach for the lamp to turn it on so my bed-stealing twin can see that I am not joking, but before my hand makes it, the obvious hits me and I let if fall to my side. I won't be able to shed any light on the

room; the lamp will be no more solid than the bedroom door I have walked through twice already.

But I'm standing here, not sinking into the floor, so maybe the lamp will be solid. The thought comes from nowhere, but before I make a move, my own very quiet laughter comes from the bed, startling me. "I told you, wait. We'll talk soon. Now leave. I can't have *my* wife hearing me talking when our room is empty. So go. Now." The words are said with force, a command, leaving no room for me to doubt the seriousness of them. But can I give in so easily? I'd like to think not.

I cannot understand what is happening, and I cannot wait for later. I want to inflict pain, and I know that whilst I cannot touch Jenny or Lucas, the flesh of this being I can touch. And if I can touch it, then I can hurt it. My hands curl into claws, claws that I move towards where I hope the throat is. I find it, and fit my hands around the neck and squeeze. But there is no strength to my hands, or the neck is resistant to my attempts. I barely make an impression—

A blast of pain runs up my arms and through my entire body, throwing me to the floor and leaving me momentarily paralysed. "Don't try and hurt me, for it won't work. And if it did, you'd only be hurting yourself. Now, for the third, and let me assure you, final time: Leave. The room. Now. We will talk when I can speak freely without worrying about being overheard. There is no need to be afraid, this is only a temporary situation."

I feel defeated. What is he—*it?*—talking about? What is temporary and how is *it* me? It has my voice and from the brief view whilst the light was on, it has my appearance, but how can it be me when I lie here, pain still radiating through my body? The confusion has overwhelmed me and I feel there is no other option but to heed the words I have been

told. I try to ignore the dejection that courses through my body at having stood down so easily, using the belief that I have no other choice, to satisfy my feeling of weakness and failure. I drag myself to my feet, ignoring the tingling that still moves throughout my body. "I'll be waiting. First thing in the morning you and I are talking." I hope my words convey the force I want them to, not the truth of my feelings of inadequacy. This *thing* has the upper hand and it seems that nothing I do will give me an advantage. There is no response, but I hear Jenny exiting Lucas's room. She heads into the bathroom. All is silent with my boy. Turning back towards the bed, I share my parting words. "If you do anything to her or my boy, you'll pay. I don't care if you are me and doing something to you will affect me. If you hurt them I won't care what harm I do myself." Even to me the words feel hollow, flat, and won't strike fear into my doppelganger. There may be no further clarity once the morning arrives, but I am hopeful that my state of mind will be clearer, and the jumbled thoughts will make a semblance of sense.

I leave the room and go sit with my son, dejection my other companion.

*   *   *

The recent events have left me in a panic and confused state, but sitting with Lucas helps to bring some calm to my mind, as he always does. I think back to the many times I have sat here while he slept, and try to push away what has transpired in the last few minutes. My normal, if not boring life, has been turned upside down and shaken up, as though it is nothing more than a snow globe, floating glitter the pieces of my reality thrown to chaos. I focus all my thoughts on Lucas

and the life I had before going to bed earlier tonight hoping it will give me the inspiration to fight through this. Whatever *this* is.

I find comfort and take immense pride in my role as a parent. I focus on that as a way to hide myself from what is going on. I was disinterested in children when I was younger, interested only in the conquest of women, never thinking of one day being with a woman for love, and wanting to create a new life together. In my early twenties, I mistreated many women, doing all I could to avoid any contact with them after we had been together for a night, and my desire had been fulfilled. Then I met Jenny through a friend, and my attitude changed drastically. Random women were no longer objects to use and discard...there would only ever be *a* woman from that point on, and her name was Jenny Ballentyne. Not long after we started dating, I was so much in love that being away from her caused a physical ache. I knew then that becoming a parent was a priority for me, joining as one and creating many children with this insanely wonderful woman. But fate, or something else, made that seemingly simple desire an almost insurmountable task.

Throughout the five months of Lucas's life I have continually expected to wake and realise that Jenny and I are, in fact, still childless; or even more gut wrenching, that we have lost our child. Whilst Jen's pregnancy with Lucas was trouble free, the years of trying for a family before that weren't. I think that we had both become convinced it would never happen. Jenny's body, until Lucas, wouldn't take to being pregnant, miscarrying five times, each one killing a part of us in the process. When we found out that we were pregnant again, we prepared ourselves for the pain of a loss that was almost guaranteed. Each day during the early pregnancy, the fear got greater that the miscarriage would happen, that it

LEIGH HAIG

was getting closer, pain ready to storm into our lives yet again. But equal to the fear was the hope that maybe this time, just maybe, it would be alright, although my mind chided any positive thoughts for it would make the hurt of loss much greater. The same hope had of course been there for the failed pregnancies, being crushed each time with the heartbreaking loss of yet another child, diminishing the optimism with subsequent pregnancies, and building a thicker wall for future self protection.

The longest pregnancy before Lucas was 11 weeks, which ended one night in front of the television with Jen suffering major stomach cramps before the blood and life of our unborn child flooded from her, our dreams and hopes of a family washed away in the fluids. We lost a baby and had to get a new sofa; and every time I looked at the sofa for the next six months, I hated it, for it was the symbol of our lost child, almost as though we had traded a life for somewhere to sit. It taunted me in nightmares, fluid stains coalescing into the face of an infant who would cry at me and ask how I could have allowed it to die.

I don't know if there is a god above, but I cursed with that miscarriage. Previously all had ended with so much less visible impact that you could almost walk away and tell yourself that it had never been, the pregnancy wasn't real. But the pool of blood and other fluids haunted me; it haunted me so much I didn't want to try for a child again. I felt that I had suffered so much. But the impact to Jenny was more than I could imagine anyone having to go through, yet she remained strong and positive, and wanted to try again. I couldn't deny her that, and I could love her with no more passion than I did during those periods. It was her strength in the constant loss and pain that kept me going. That kept *us* going.

# SHADES OF REALITY

Once the pregnancy with Lucas had passed 11 weeks, the fear, whilst increasing, was matched with optimism and hope. But the next strike against us came a week later with a high probability of Down syndrome based on the blood work and nuchal fold test. At 41, Jenny's age, was working against us. We agreed against the amniocentesis test to get a conclusive result; we did not want to risk a miscarriage when this was something that already hovered over our heads. We simply prepared for the possibility our child would be born with Down's...if the pregnancy got that far. The curses to the god that may be above turned to prayers of hope that this time, this unexpected pregnancy would be the one, and our little baby would be healthy. Which he was.

But now, after what has happened tonight, I have to wonder if my fears of losing my son have come true, but in a way I could never have imagined.

Chapter 5

After an hour or so of sitting on the floor—I had tried the sofa, but had fallen right through it, yet I can sit on the floor...why?—and staring at the dark TV screen looking for answers, I hear Lucas cry out, blaring his organic alarm clock wake up wail.

Instinct takes over as I rise and walk down the short hallway to his room. On the way, Lucas's cries start to muffle as though his little face is pressed into the mattress. I quicken my step, a panic that he is going to suffocate urging me along.

I had sat with Lucas for several hours after leaving my room, the rhythm of his sleep helping to soothe my jumbled mind. Talking to him and telling him how much his mum and I loved him and how as a family we were going to be okay. When I had nothing left to say and no feelings of tiredness, I left Lucas, and headed to our small living room, looking briefly into the darkened bedroom and feeling sick at my inability to explain what was happening, or to do anything about it. I spent the rest of the night gazing at the television, my mind as blank as its screen.

Now, I walk through the open doorway into Lucas's room—early morning light pushing away the darkness—and see him in the arms of the other me. But not in a nurturing embrace. Lucas's mouth and nose are covered by the other's mouth. The rage of last night instantly returns and I move towards the two of them, hands fisted. I swing both arms in wild arcs, aiming for no part specifically, but trying to avoid Lucas. My fists hit the other: one in the stomach, the other in the shoulder. I quickly strike again and again. My fists

connect, but I hit him with as much effectiveness as a pillow hitting a brick wall.

He snakes his hand out and grips my throat. I *feel* fingers of steel encircling it, an electric agony sparking through my body, my vision wavering, white dots dancing. My body sags, and the pressure on my throat eases enough that I am able to pull away.

I look to where he stands and see him now holding Lucas to his chest, no longer trying to suffocate my boy. "It's not what you may be thinking, so relax. I know it's morning now, but it's not yet time for us to speak." His words are whispered, eyes shifting to the door behind me as they are spoken.

I am unable to respond; I stand still, staring at my mirror image (he's even wearing the same blue dressing gown I find myself still wearing, despite trying numerous times to remove it). The me I see carries the same expanding waistline that I have been trying to contain since Lucas's arrival, but which seems to be defying my attempts. He has a full head of shortly cropped brown hair with too much grey coming through, and close set brown eyes; a rather unremarkable face, but one I have gotten used to. Though looking at it now, outside of a mirror, gives me the creeps for I am not seeing it in reflection, but how it appears to everyone else. A way I should never be seeing it.

Then I hear the toilet flushing. I look over my shoulder, and watch as Jenny enters the room, blond hair a mess, but a huge smile on her face: the same smile she always has for Lucas.

"How's my little soldier?" she asks as she walks through me—once again causing agony where our bodies merge; I step backwards to lessen the time we share the same physical space—arms out to take him from what she believes to be her

husband. I stand like a statue and watch the three of them, knowing it should be the three of *us*.

Jenny takes Lucas into her arms. He *gurgles* and *ahs* at her, and receives a warm hug for his response. Seeing the love, but not being involved in it, saddens me. I turn and walk from the room, dejection still with me, leaving the happy family. I wonder what has caused this, what will happen next, and just when will I find out what the hell is going on. Asking questions right now will serve me no value for my twin made it clear he will not talk to me whilst Jen is within hearing distance.

I return to the living room where there is enough of dawn's light for me to see. I hold my hands in front of my face expecting to be able to see through them, but they look solid. I spread the lapels of the dressing gown apart and look at my naked chest, which also looks solid. Rapping my knuckles against it produces both feeling and noise. I am solid, yet I am able to pass through things. Yet another question that keeps fear circling my every thought, and that I add to the growing list for me to seek an answer to.

Chapter 6

Later that day, it being a Saturday, having moped around and watched someone that is not me masquerade as me, interacting with my family whilst I am not able to do a damn thing about it, Jenny announces she's taking Lucas for a walk. We'd often go out together, enjoying some fresh air as a family, or sometimes just Lucas and I giving us father and son bonding time, and Jen some much deserved *her* time. Even though I won't actually be with her, I have my doubts as to the other's intent and decide I'll go along. But this is halted when Jenny asks me—him, but to her, it is me—if I'm coming.

I'm standing off to the side when this is asked. I turn to him and watch, waiting for his reply. Instead of looking at Jenny he turns his head to face me, staring directly into my eyes. "You know what, I think I may just hang around here and be with myself for a bit." The tone of voice and direct eye contact with me makes the meaning of the words obvious: I am to stay here with him. This will be the time for revelation.

As he helps Jenny get Lucas ready for the walk, nerves start to flutter. I'm not sure if the reaction is from a fear of what is going to happen, or the uncertainty of finding out what is going on. Despite the need to know that burned at me all night long, could knowing cause me more harm than good, strike fear where ignorance offers a comforting layer? *I need to know*, I tell myself. *Ignorance is not an option.* While I continue to ponder this, the other me comes up from behind and puts a hand on my shoulder. I jerk away expecting pain, but there is nothing beyond the light touch

of his hand.

"Easy, bucko. I'm not here to hurt you, and now it's question and answer time. But first—" he walks to the stereo and turns it on, Pearl Jam launching from the speakers "—some background noise. Can't have the wife coming home and hearing me talking to myself. She may question her decision in marrying me." I turn to look his way, and he gives me a wink, a small smirk playing across the lips.

"So, why don't you take a seat?" His right hand gestures towards the sofa and then he chuckles, using my voice, but definitely not my laugh. "Don't fret. Just my sense of humour added to your body. Why don't we both sit on the floor, that way you don't feel belittled in any way."

He moves to a clear place on the floor and sits down, using his hand to indicate I should take a seat next to him. I move, but keep my distance, not going as near as indicated, and sit down, worried by the close proximity to him. A fear of oneself is an irrational feeling to have, but I convince myself to view the other me as something other than myself.

I swivel my head around looking at everything but the person sitting next to me, as though I'm seeing this room and its contents for the first time. The entertainment unit against the wall with our audio visual equipment, a CD stand off to the left. The curtains are open, sunlight streaming in, dust motes dancing and wavering in the light. On the wall above the sofa hangs a photo from our honeymoon, a moment that I'd rather be reliving than going through what today has become. His voice breaks the spell, and I finally turn to look at him.

"We don't want to take all day. Jen will only be gone for a half hour. She rarely takes Lucas out for any longer than that." He is telling me what I already know, of course, what I have experienced and lived. As though he has been watching

our lives, or as though...as though he *is* me, and he has my memories. I shiver at the thought.

I find my voice, which croaks for the first few words. "I woke up to see to Lucas and nothing happened. But here you are and, and well, I have no idea what's going on. Or why." I don't know where to go with this. I now have the opportunity to find out what is happening and I feel too confused to make the time work for me. The questions, the fears and thoughts that have plagued me since early morning are absent now that I have the chance to air them. So I am thankful when he starts talking without further prompting.

"I've already told you, and it's your choice to believe it or not, but I am not here to hurt you or your family. I am here to survive, and in doing so, no harm will come to anyone living here." My own brown eyes look at me, staking me to where I sit. I try to look for a lie, but can't see anything, and am not really sure what to look for; even when looking at my own face, I am not able to discern what tics or signs would betray a lie or mistruth. But neither can I see anything that makes me confident that what is being said is the truth. I open my mouth to ask a question, but he continues before I can speak.

"You're not the first to go through what is happening here. I do this often, and when I leave, lives go on as if I was never here. And indeed it will here, too. For you see, once I go, you'll return to being you. I'll leave you with memories of the next few days so you won't even have a gap in your life. While I'm here, I will be you, and continue your life as if there is nothing different. I have your memories and I have your knowledge. I'll go into work tomorrow and manage that supermarket in the same way you would. To everyone I interact with, they will think it is you they are talking to and working with."

I speak up, the first of my questions rolling from my tongue as *Better Man* plays on the stereo. "How long? How long will I be like this...and what is this? Why can I see my family and house, but touch none of them? Yet I can touch you, and you can touch me. How?" I find I am leaning forward, like a child eager to hear the next part of an exciting story, but the reason could not be further from that.

"A week, maybe eight days. It all depends on how long my..." He pauses, pursing his lips in thought. "My rejuvenation, shall we call it, takes. It varies but normally a week. As to your other questions, well, you're here, but not really. When I shifted into your body, you were moved to a slightly different reality. From where you are now, there is effectively a one way mirror back to where you were, allowing you to see what is happening, but not allowing you to interact, or those still there to see or hear you. I on the other hand am a part of both realities. This allows you and I to interact, whilst I can also be you. The pain you feel when passing through a living thing from this world is due to the closeness of the realities, and the impact of two living things trying to occupy the same space in the respective realms. My advice is to avoid others completely. Safest for you to stay in the house until this is done. I cannot state that enough: don't go wandering when I am working, even if it is to stay near your wife. Out there—" his hand gestures towards the window and the bright day that exists outside "—will only bring you pain and potential harm, so avoid it."

I hear the words, but they bounce through my mind, rattling around and not falling into place. Two way mirrors? Other realities? He's talking science fiction, something that isn't real, or couldn't be. Could it?

As I am trying to slot the words into the right place, something that was said hits me. "Rejuvenation? What do

you mean by that? And how come I can walk through things, yet I am able to sit here on the floor and not pass through it?" I know there are more important things to discuss, but this fact has been troubling me for reasons I cannot fully grasp. I should just accept it for what it is, but I wonder if it in some way ties to the bigger picture of what is happening.

A sad smile crosses the face I'm staring into, the same face I see every morning when I shave. I see the scar under my right eye from a bike accident when I was seven but today it, and the rest of the face, is as foreign as another person altogether.

"Second question first. You would not understand the answer, and in all honesty I cannot do the question justice." There is a long pause, and I wonder if he has in fact said all he will on this topic, but then, after looking into the distance, he continues. "The ground of both realities is identical. With the floor coverings being laid directly onto the ground in this reality, it becomes another layer to the ground of the reality you now exist in. It really comes down to the density of the ground. The ground beneath the floor is solid and it brings firmness to the floor coverings here. But if the density of the ground below where you stand was to reduce, and the thickness became less than three feet, you would likely pass through the floor. If this were a two storey house, you would not be able to go upstairs as the floor would no longer be on solid ground."

I shake my head in bewilderment, almost regretting that I felt the need to ask, and now feel dumb not being able to make sense of what I've been told. "I guess you're right. I think I can understand what you're saying, but I don't suppose it matters, does it?" I gaze into my own brown eyes, and he shakes his head slightly.

"No, it doesn't matter. But what does matter and is

more important is your first question and what I meant by rejuvenation. The reality in which you sit now holds few of us. We are an older being that needs youth to survive. When we slip into the body and life of another, we are doing so to share the life force of a child—"

I am up and moving at him, a fire in my belly, fists clenched, all thoughts of the previous attack and pain set aside. As soon as he mentions life force and child, the image of him smothering Lucas this morning roars into my mind, followed by a red mist that calls for bloodshed. He shakes his head, almost a gesture of pity, and then he's on his feet. Hands reach out and grab mine, halting me from taking a swing. The force of the hold also stops my forward momentum, but the burning pain felt this morning is not repeated.

My arms struggle against his grip. "Let me go you bastard!" I yell. "How dare you enter my body and my life and steal anything from my child. He is everything to me, and if I die trying, so help me I will end this."

He is obviously allowing me my rage for as I finish speaking, the pain strikes, and once my arms are released I fall to the tiled floor, falling *through* the coffee table. Agony surges through my body even though there is no longer contact between the two of us.

His words reach me through the haze that has become my mind. "I didn't want to do that, but you really do need to watch that temper." I slide out from under the coffee table, moving away from him, but watching warily. I look at the face, a face that even though I have lived with it for 43 years, is one that I am beginning to loathe. It has become a mask, something worn by another, that is shielding the truth from me. "I told you I am not here to hurt anyone. I am not stealing anything from your boy. As he breathes out, parts of his youth, a part that I use to survive comes on his breath. I

am simply taking what is expelled, and nothing more."

The windows rattle as a gust of wind blows against them. I ignore the noise and continue to stare at him, looking for the truth, hoping to find it, for I desperately want to believe. But can I? And if I don't, what can I do, anyway?

"Okay. You win," I tell him.

I have more to say, but he cuts me off, shaking his head. "I don't win. There is nothing to win beyond I get to survive." The voice carries what I can almost feel is sympathy. Or is it pity? If only I could read my own voice!

"So until you're done here, I what, sit around and wait?" I ask.

"That's my recommendation. You've felt the pain when you cross paths with another living creature, so do you really want to leave the safety of your home? Safer to just hang here and you can watch over me for I can see in your eyes and body language that you don't trust me. And I can understand that; no one has ever trusted me at first, so why would you?"

"What about this?" I ask pointing at the dressing gown more often worn by my wife than I. "Am I stuck in this until you're done here?" I am rewarded with the first hearty laugh I have heard boom from my own body since it was hijacked.

"Unfortunately what you were wearing at the time of crossing over will remain with you until you return; those clothes are now a part of *what* you are. Which is a bit of bad luck." And he laughs again, shaking his head from obvious amusement, which leads me to see the funny side. I stifle a laugh, but it soon escapes and we briefly share the moment. For the first time since I tried to return to bed earlier in the morning, I feel somewhat at peace, only a small trace of fear present.

I sit back and listen to more *Pearl Jam*, and think about

what I have been told, trying to rationalise and find a way to believe it.

Chapter 7

For the next six days I wander the house, keeping a close watch on the other whilst he's at home, and looking out for Jen and Lucas regardless of where he is.

Every morning and once or twice a day when the opportunity presents, The Bastard—for that is how I've come to think of him for what he is doing to me, casting me aside and living my life while I can do nothing but watch on—will place his mouth over Lucas's face, in the same manner I saw on that first morning. Each time I witness this, rage builds, but I take no action against him (other than turning my back, though out of sight does not make it out of mind), a mixture of fear of the repercussions against me, and the hope that what I have been told is true, that no harm is being done to my son. I monitor Lucas closely to see if there is anything happening to him, but he seems unchanged, no worse for the action. Despite my hatred of what I see *him* doing, the lack of impact to Lucas offers me some salvation, a life preserver that I cling to.

I have spoken to Jenny every day, telling her about this crazy situation and hoping that if I speak to her enough, something will reach her. But for all the talking, I may as well have been talking to a mannequin. Every day I have reached out to her and tried to make physical contact, but spikes of pain to my body are her only way of responding. I've stood next to her whilst she looks in the mirror in the hope she will see me, but I am not even visible to myself. I also try Lucas, but whether I am talking to him or staring into his face, he never shows any sign of hearing or seeing his dad. I really am lost to my family, and hold out for the

time when this is over.

It is during the evening of the sixth day, I decide I need to get out of the house. Jenny is having one of her moments where she wants to be held and I know where it will eventually lead once Lucas is down for the night. And I don't want to be in the house while someone else takes my wife to bed and makes love to her. The pain is enough seeing her daily and not being able to touch or interact with her. To see (or hear) her in bed would feel like the ultimate betrayal, though not one I could ever hold against her.

Like a well trained child, I approach The Bastard to tell him I'll be going out. He and Jenny are sitting on the couch watching the news while dinner is in the oven. Jenny nurses Lucas in her right arm, her left around The Bastard's waist, head resting on his shoulder. His right hand is caressing her upper thigh, the foreplay already started. He is looking happy and relaxed, a contented smile on his face, the Sunday through Thursday working week over.

"I'm going out. I—"

"No!" The reaction is harsh, The Bastard sitting up and taking his hand from Jen's leg. Her arm falls from his waist, her reaction to his sudden outburst equal to mine: shock. For me, it is a shock that he has reacted to me in her presence. She is the first to speak up about it, mouth hanging agape.

"What was that all about? You having a private conversation with someone I don't know about?" If only Jen could hear my spontaneous laughter. The Bastard does hear, and gives me a glowering look, one that could stop a charging elephant. Jenny often told me I had a mean look when I wanted, and seeing it for the first time staring back at me, I have to agree. It almost makes me forget the reason behind the look.

"Now that's a silly thing to say." He fidgets as he speaks, but Jen is only half watching, also interested in the current story on the news telecast, so does not witness the momentary discomfort.

"Is it, good buddy?" This is an opportunity too good to let go. "Sure you weren't talking to someone like, oh let's say, me? Seems like I scared you at the mention of me going—"

He abruptly stands from the couch, giving Jen and Lucas a pat each on the head as if they're a damn pet, and then announcing loudly, to silence my tormenting, "I forgot to tell Rob at work a couple of things I need him to do tonight. You know how frustrated I get when I forget things."

A smile crosses Jenny's face, as I see she has easily bought it. "Don't be so hard on yourself, Nigel. You work hard, so forgetting a thing or two isn't the end of the world."

I know she can't hear me, but I talk over the top of her anyway. "That's bullshit, Jen. Don't let him get away with it. Keep pushing, make him crack and I may get back a bit sooner." But of course she doesn't even know I'm gone. I've become a third wheel watching my own life from the outside, with an underlying fear that tinges everything. I have to believe what I have been told, but there is still doubt, a doubt that I don't know how to alleviate. I'm thrust into a position of believe and accept, or not believe but accept the consequences of any mistruths that have been told. This internal debate has harrowed me the past six days as I try to find truth or flaw, and a path of action I can take. But no matter what, I feel powerless.

My arm is grabbed, and I am yanked from my thoughts. I've missed part of the conversation. "...and let him know what I need done, then I'll be back and get dinner out of the oven." I look over my shoulder as I am dragged away and see Jen has already turned her full attention back to the news.

LEIGH HAIG

Even though he hasn't done his thing with the pain, I'm still unhappy at his actions. "Hold up there, liar."

I continue to be dragged through the kitchen, with a detour to allow The Bastard to grab the cordless phone from the holder on the wall. My protests continue to be ignored as our journey terminates in the master bedroom.

I'm thrown to the bed, but go right through it and hit the floor on my back, pain radiating from my spine to my extremities.

I hear the beep-beep-beep of the phone's keypad being pushed and set my bafflement of the situation aside. I momentarily wonder if The Bastard was telling the truth about the need to talk to Rob, the night manager at work. Sitting up and emerging through the mattress I see him standing against the wall, holding the phone at his side. I see a glimpse of pure hatred, eyes narrowed and mouth a snarl, but it's quickly wiped away by a more neutral and passive expression.

"Now listen to me. You do not want to leave this house if you want to stay safe. I hadn't said anything in detail before at the risk of worrying you, but I think you need to know. If you care about your family the way I know you do—" he says this tapping his finger against his temple "—you'll be staying inside." I watch him closely and notice his inability to look at me while he speaks, his eyes shifting around the room. "It's dangerous. The reality you currently exist in is not empty. There are...how should I say this...other creatures that, unlike me, survive through—" He halts at the sound of approaching footsteps, and raises the phone to his ear. I hear Jenny's voice cooing to Lucas as she approaches.

"So that's all I need Rob. Appreciate your help in taking care of that and I'll see you Sunday afternoon." He pauses as though listening to someone on the other end, a someone I

know isn't there. "Great. Bye." Removing the phone from his ear and hitting the disconnect button, he turns as Jen stops at the doorway, Lucas cuddled to her chest.

"All fixed, dear?" she asks. "Should I get dinner out?"

He has turned away from me, but I can hear the smile in his voice—my voice. "Yep, he's a good man and will sort it out. And yeah, let's get that dinner ready. I'm starving."

"You lying phony, prick! How dare you continue to masquerade as me," I yell at him. "And what about the danger that supposedly exists? Aren't you the biggest goddamn danger here? Pretending to be a man when you're nothing but a beast?" I haven't believed a word of what he has just said. It felt contrived, said for someone else's benefit, not mine. But if that is the case, what is at the heart of the lie, and what does it mean for all of the other reassurances I've been given this past week?

As Jen turns and heads back towards the kitchen, The Bastard leaps at me, snarling briefly, holding the phone high as if to bludgeon me with it. I involuntarily step back. "We're through here," he whispers. "Take my warning seriously. You don't know what's out there, and trust me, it will be stupidity on your part to try and find out. If I get the chance later, I'll fill you in. But for now rest easy and stay in the house. I'll be done soon...if not tomorrow morning then I'm pretty sure the next. But for now, I have dinner to eat."

And as quickly as he came at me, he exits the room.

"Fine. Go and get your dinner ready and eat with *my* family. Bastard."

Chapter 8

The Bastard and Jen have been in bed for a couple of hours, having retired early, the noise of their passion having silenced a while ago (though the seething inside me lingers, as does the regret that I somehow forced myself to hear it, for some masochistic reason I am unaware of). I feel sure that he should be safely asleep. It's time to leave.

I exit the house silently, gliding right through the front door, a benefit of my current state. Ever since The Bastard's earlier outburst, I've had it in my mind to clear out, go and explore a little, albeit cautiously, his warnings not completely dismissed as lies. My mind has been turning so many things over, his reaction having caused me to analyse and wonder at the truth of all that I've been told, pulling it apart and looking for inconsistencies. But with the doubt has come a terrifying reality of the alternative, for if I have been lied to, what is being hidden, what truth requires the lie? His story, or what he was able to briefly share of why I shouldn't leave, smelt of fabrication. It was more likely he didn't want me to leave for his benefit, not mine. But again...*why*? If there is the slightest chance that staying in the house has the potential to cause Lucas or Jenny harm, a harm that I could prevent by getting out and exploring, then be damned if I'd stay. I'd take my chances of any action he may choose to force upon me should my disobedience be revealed.

Since being in this altered state I've gotten used to the removal of the boundaries of my living self. I haven't slept since waking up to settle Lucas; nor have I felt tired in any way. I tested my ability to be energetic without the normal aching body and shortness of breath normally accompanying

exercise, and found I could be active for hours without even puffing. Sadly though, this new ability (and lack of eating) has done nothing to fight off the middle-aged spread carried with me to my phantom body.

Having slid through the door without a second thought, I look down at my flip-flopped feet and Jenny's dressing gown and give a little shrug. I may look stupid, but no one will be seeing me.

Without a real plan, but wanting to make the most of the night and be back before The Bastard awakens, I decide that wherever I am going, I'll get there quicker if I run. So I start to run, leaving my house and family behind, hopefully not for the last time.

*   *   *

The night is beautiful and clear, the sky awash with a hundred pinpricks of light. Wind gently tickles at the trees, the undoubtedly cold air having no effect on me. After what feels like thirty minutes, the occasional grumble of passing cars barely registering, and seeing little foot traffic to avoid, I arrive at the fringes of the city. I have run at full steam—or as full steam as can be achieved when wearing cheap hotel slippers and carrying too much weight—and am not in the least exhausted. If anything, I feel partly energised, the great outdoors helping to lift the oppression that has cast its shawl over me this last week.

As I ran, I had no awareness as to my eventual destination, the city never being in my mind. But now that I am here, it seems the logical part of me was leading my movements, for what better place to go when trying to...? The thought is left unfinished. Now that I have stopped moving, I really have no idea what I am trying to achieve in tonight's

expedition.

Standing here now, with the lights and passing foot and vehicular traffic I wonder exactly what I am going to achieve. What can I possibly find that will explain, one way or another, what is going on, and what danger I and my family may be in? A feeling of dejection hits me, and a sad realisation that I am not in control, and never have been. The fate of those I hold dearer than anything else are at the mercy of something I cannot understand, and that I can do nothing about.

I slowly move deeper into the city, making exaggerated movements to avoid running into anyone, or allowing them to pass through me. I ponder how much we rely on others to avoid us as we avoid them when in busy areas, for I have to work much harder to stay out of people's way now that I cannot be seen.

Although I cannot feel it, I imagine the buzz I get when visiting the city late at night. The sense of excitement from those around me, with the constant underlying current of fear that at any moment alcohol fuelled violence will break out, shattering all fun demonstrating the ugliness to which a night out can become. What I do feel are pangs of jealousy as I watch friends and couples out for a night on the town: going to and from movies, talking about the wonderful meals they've just eaten, making their way from one pub to another. All bundled up against the obvious cold of this Thursday night, of which I feel nothing. I get lost in my jealousy, wanting to be here with Jen, someone at home baby-sitting Lucas. Part of this desire comes from the separation I have felt from my family in the last week, but also the loss of the time Jen and I have been able to spend alone, since Lucas's arrival. He means the world to me of course, but since he was born Jen and I have had no time to our self, no

more nice dinners, no movies, nothing but loving and caring for him.

As soon as the thoughts pass through my mind a bolt of shame strikes me. I've also been so absorbed in my thoughts that I have lost awareness of the goings on around me. I am slammed back to my version of reality when two friends joking with each other walk right through me. My shame is quickly replaced by an agony that runs through my body, as though every cell is on fire. As they complete their passage through me, I fall to my knees, the pain and stress taking something from my body that the run hadn't.

I hear a lone voice coming from behind me, the words lost, and struggle to my feet to avoid more searing pain, but am halted by the pressure of a hand around my arm. I turn, a sudden sinking feeling, knowing that The Bastard has followed me and is ready to extract revenge for my betrayal of his advice. But neither the face I turn to see nor the voice that speaks to me, are mine.

"Come on, let me give you a hand." The voice is quiet, sad almost, and there is a slight accent I cannot place. Something European or middle eastern, perhaps.

"Thanks. I–" Realisation slaps me in the face and my words dry up: this person can see me, and is able to grasp my arm, not pass right through me! I get a good look at the newcomer. He is wearing striped flannel pyjamas over his tall thin build, with slippered feet. His face is long and thin, mid thirtyish with side burns. His mouth forms a weary smile.

"You're like...like me." The words explode from my mouth, my confusion hitting a new high. My arm is let go and I allow it to fall to my side.

"I am. My name's Hasad." He extends his hand, the smile turning from weary to warm. I reach out and with some trepidation take his hand in mine. After two quick

pumps, we release hands, and I look closely at Hasad; I need to know: friend or foe? I will have to watch closely and be on guard, but I am willing—praying—that Hasad proves to be a friend. And one with information that will help.

"I'm Nigel." I pause, confusion limiting my vocabulary. "Look, I said you're like me, but I have no idea what that means. Please tell me you can help me understand what's happening?" I feel a glimmer of hope sparking deep in my gut, one that might light a fire to burn away all doubt and mystery of the last few days. I know it is premature, but I am willing it to be true.

Hasad suddenly reaches his hand out, grabbing my arm, pushing me onto the road. *What the hell?* I am about to retaliate when a person walks past where I was only moments before, and I realise Hasad's action was simply to move me from their path.

"Thanks," I say, relaxing my fingers from the fists they have formed. I move myself into the gutter, moving further from the passing cars, their occupants done for the day and heading home.

"That's okay. I've been living like this for a long time. I almost have a sixth sense for approaching harm. Helps that I have suffered a lot of pain in the 20 odd years I have been like this."

"Twenty years?" I ask, shocked and scared by this revelation. The thought of not being able to hold or share moments with my family for such a time horrifies me. Could it be that The Bastard's talk of it being a week or so is a lie? But why make such a false claim? What possible benefits could there be in misleading me? And again, what of the rest of the things he has told me? These questions spiral through my mind, but I am brought back to the present with more words from Hasad.

# SHADES OF REALITY

"Yes, but let's get off the road and away from the foot traffic. You can then tell me your story and I'll see what I can do to help." He starts to turn, and then, much quieter: "Saved many people in my years, but not all, which still leaves an emptiness that aches."

"Hang on." I reach out and grab both his arms to still his movement, no longer aware of my surroundings, or of the cars swishing by. "What do you mean 'saved many people'? Who is in danger? And what *is* the danger? Please, tell me." My fingers tighten their grip.

Hasad looks sad. I am not sure what my words have done to him, but they seem to have caused some inner pain—the man I first met barely seconds ago replaced with one haunted by demons I cannot see. "I understand your concern, but a few more minutes won't be a problem. Now let's go, the longer we stand here the longer it will be before we can talk."

Since I am the rookie here and have all to gain from Hasad, I concede to his wish. "Okay. Lead the way." With a nod, he turns and walks back the way from which he came. With no other option, I follow.

Chapter 9

He leads me through a warren of back streets and alleys, every new one we turn down darker than the last. I have tried to question Hasad, a seed of distrust germinating. I have not seen anyone walk *through* him, and he is walking outside, not using the ability to walk through things, so I have no idea if he belongs in the real world; is he really like me and isolated from contact, or is he like The Bastard, straddling both realities? I worry that my relief at having someone find me, someone with *substance* in the reality I live in, has blinded me to the dangers he may present. But this thought is always followed with the question of does Hasad present more of a danger to me than if I was still at home, under the watchful eye of The Bastard? For I really have no inclination as to exactly what The Bastard is all about, as much as I want to believe that what he has told me is true.

Eventually Hasad comes to a stop in front of an old steel doorway, graffiti scrawled across it and the surrounding wall, the writing illegible scribbles with no artistic merit; idiotic tagging by mindless youths. The building to which it is a part of, is old and looks like it's ready to fall to the ground, its bluestone walls looking less than sturdy. To the right of the doorway is a broken window, sharp glass shards attached to the frame like a giant's teeth. Something has been placed over the window from behind, probably to keep out the homeless and young who would use the building for their own, more than likely, seedy purposes.

Although there is very little light in this area I see enough to recognise the building as the old Lleyland textile factory, which was closed down in the late '80s and has

remained vacant since then.

"Sorry, but I lost the key. Hope you don't mind." Hasad's words bring me back to the now, and with a chuckle, he steps through the door and vanishes from my sight. This act, although simple, gives me a shot of confidence. I have not seen The Bastard move through anything, but Hasad just walked through a steel door. It gives me hope that he is *only* in the same world as I, and not crossing between the two as is the *other* me. Not wanting to lose him, or give him any time to plan a trap (a spurt of confidence is not enough to wash away all doubt), I enter the building.

The darkness of the interior makes the minimal light outside feel like we were in the middle of the day, not sometime between midnight and dawn. I listen for the sounds of footfalls, but with Hasad being like me, a man not really of this world, I hear nothing from his movement. Absolute silence, for there is no noise from the streets seeping into this dark place, no rumbling of engines or distant laughter carried across the night air. I imagine it must smell of must and old machinery, but I have no ability to inhale the aromas of the past which are surely here.

"Hasad, hello?" I call out to the darkness, my own voice startling me with its volume, and a distinct hollowness without a returning echo.

"Right here, on the floor." The voice comes to me from my left, very close. "Unfortunately being shades of another reality leaves us unable to interact with physical objects in this world so I cannot provide any lighting for us. Come, sit." I use the sound of his voice as a guide to locate him, and sit on the hard floor.

"Alright we're here. But why? Why have we had to come to this place? What couldn't you have told me on the street that you can tell me now?" I can hear the anger in my voice,

the frustration at not getting answers, and I try to calm myself down. I don't need answers to those questions, as there are more important things to discuss; they were asked more as an outlet for my growing frustration.

Before Hasad wastes time answering these questions, I ask a pertinent one. "So tell me what you meant earlier about saving people, but not all. My wife and son, are they in danger?"

"Yes, I am sure you need to know. You must be curious, but also fearful. I can recall both of these affecting me when I had the same thing happen all those years ago."

I want to reach out and find him in the blackness that holds us both, and shake an answer loose, but I'm once again forced into calmness, for I do not want to lose this potential ally through my own impatience.

Instead of answering my questions, Hasad begins a tale. "I had gotten up to use the bathroom one night, surprised that my little girl hadn't woken for her feed. After finishing up, I returned to bed to find someone already lying there. But I'm sure you know how it goes."

I nod my head in agreement, despite knowing the gesture cannot be seen.

I wait, and eventually, he continues. "But for me, it differed in the ending to so many others, and the way it is supposed to. I was told that within eight days I would be back in my body and my life would return to the way it was. I could never in my heart believe that everything was as it seemed, but I hoped. On the seventh day, the thing that stole my life, was in a car crash. My body was destroyed, but the thing lived for a short while after the accident. I was at home with my wife and child, though they didn't know I was there. I hadn't left the house since *it* arrived and stole my body. I didn't know at the time, but I felt an incredible pull as the

accident happened, one that dragged me away from the house as though I was caught by a fishing line and the fisherman was reeling me in." Hasad pauses again, his voice having grown heavy, grief tinging his accent. I can picture him sitting close to me, his eyes focusing on the past.

The silence stretches on. I listen closely for noise, wondering if he is still here. Just as I worry that I've been abandoned, his voice booms from the darkness, a strength to it that I hadn't heard previously. "I was pulled back to my body, my flesh and blood self still in the mangled wreck of my car. I remember the blood everywhere, leaking onto the road alongside fluids from the car, the shuffling of para-medics to try and save me...to save my body. I then felt a tickling in my mind and was drawn closer to the smashed body, barely recognisable as myself. I passed through a paramedic, the tug ever there, along with the blinding pain. But then the tug stopped, as though the line dragging me in had been severed. That was when I heard the paramedic pronounce me dead."

The power of the story leaves me feeling empty. To witness one's own death and continue to live in a manner that allows you to remember the event and see the details in your own mind must be a terrible thing. "I am...I'm so sorry. That must have been...I don't know. Terrible just seems inade-quate." The words mean little but they are heartfelt.

"Thank you, Nigel, but really, it was a long time ago. My body died in 1986, so I've had many years to grieve and move on. In a manner, I still live, though it would have been nice to have a decent set of clothes to be wearing for eternity." Hasad lets out a laugh that I immediately find infectious, my own laughter momentarily giving me a feeling of comfort. I know the attire I currently wear is no better and not one I would want to be stuck with. At least we are

invisible to the ridicule we would surely get in the *real* world.

"So that is what happened. After the intruder had finished what *it* was there to do, I should have swapped back into my body and gone on with life, as changed as it would have been. But my body ceased to live, killing the thing within it and leaving me trapped like this. I have since learned—for my life has become singularly focused on achieving complete understanding of everything concerning the takeover—that the pull I felt that brought me to the accident was *its* attempt to escape my dying remains. To leave the body, *it* must bring the owner back into it, but my body died before the transaction could be completed, leaving me stranded in where we are now."

Hearing that the being that currently sleeps with my wife can be killed fills me with hope. Though there is still some doubt that killing *him* is something I want to do, the end I need to achieve. I want to share my story with Hasad now and see how he can help me; see how to get my life back. There is nothing I want more than to hold my wife and son close and make sure that I am the best husband and father I can be. But first, I have a question I need to ask, to give me closure to his story. "What about your wife and child?" It strikes me as strange that he has a wife and child, but chooses to hide in this warehouse.

"I no longer know. A year after I died, my wife moved back to Turkey. I didn't let them out of my sight, though seeing your loved one mourn your loss is devastating. I was by her side as she made the arrangements to sell our possessions, sell the house, and so on. It broke my heart, both seeing her distress at being here alone, and knowing that I would soon lose her. Being able to walk through objects has advantages, but it means you're stuck here, not able to board a plane or ship. And I've tried both trying to

make my way back to Turkey, to find them." His voice, previously booming, has decreased to something barely above a whisper. The thought of a loved one's life becoming nothing more than possessions to be sorted through and discarded horrifies me. Neither Jen nor Lucas should be forced to endure that now, or anytime in the distant future. I won't allow it.

I am not sure if he has finished sharing his story, so I sit in silence waiting, pondering what I have just heard. Having listened through his telling, I feel wrong sharing my own story, as though it would be demeaning to the experiences Hasad has been through. But I have been brought here to share my story. I feel cold thinking it, but his family has been lost, nothing can be done for them. Mine are still here, and I need him to focus on helping me save them.

Before he speaks again, a loud crash reverberates throughout the entire building, echoing off the walls. I launch to my feet, fearing that I have allowed myself to become trapped whilst listening to a fabricated story. I imagine a hundred Hasad's all rushing towards me through the darkness, ready to tear me apart, some sick game that is played in the reality I currently exist in.

I back away, heading in the direction I think the door is, but Hasad speaks, his words halting me, the calmness in his voice providing some reassurance. "Probably just the rats. The building is full of them."

Feeling some guilt at my negative thoughts towards him, I take a couple of steps back to roughly where I had been sitting and drop to the floor. The doubt and confusion mingle creating havoc with my thoughts. If I can so quickly turn my trust of Hasad into mistrust, then I mustn't hold much faith in him.

"So now I need to know your story, Nigel, to see what

we can do for you." His voice floats from the darkness.

I open my mouth and start at the beginning. Throughout my story there is no sound whatsoever save for my own voice. It is as though I am alone and talking to myself, but I don't stop, the telling of it almost cathartic, bringing the craziness into reality. I describe in detail the actions witnessed of The Bastard against my son, the covering of his mouth and nose, and provide—using the exact words where I remember them—the intent of those actions as told to me. I think I hear a sigh as I detail this, but I am so absorbed that I talk through it, only half consciously registering the noise. At one point I stand up and pace in the darkness, my hands gesticulating though no one can see them. I walk back and forth trying not to stray too far from the spot where Hasad sits. On one return walk I accidentally kick him with my foot, breaking my narrative to briefly apologise.

I eventually wrap the tale up with my arrival into the city and Hasad's finding me. "I had no awareness of where I was going the entire time I was running. I don't know if I was looking for somewhere to try and escape from my confusion, or somewhere that I could find answers, though I never really believed there would be a place for either. Now, I have some hope." A meagre smile touches the corner of my mouth, but I choose not to say that the hope is matched with equal measures of doubt and scepticism, though I do feel the story he has shared is genuine. But is it a false hope because of my greater distrust of The Bastard?

The anger (was there fear there also? Yes, I think so) The Bastard showed when I mentioned leaving the house returns to me and I have to know if Hasad can make anything of it. "Why would The Bastard have reacted the way he did when I mentioned leaving the house? I mean he literally blew up, and was adamant that I not leave."

"I find your naming of this thing to be very appropriate, and it brings a smile to my face. I wonder if deep down you knew the truth of its intentions. I did not trust the one that ruined my life, and called it *Yalan* which is Turkish for 'lie,' for that is what I knew it was doing to me.

"But we have more important things to discuss. Firstly, you were drawn into the city towards me, and I was drawn here to find you. As you got closer, I could feel your presence. In this shifted reality we inhabit, we are somehow drawn towards others also here. It took me a while to notice, but there is a gentle pull that will direct your movements, bringing you closer to another shade. I cannot explain how this happens, or even why, but that it does, well, that means we can work together to makes things right.

"As for The Bastard's reaction when you announced you were going to leave the house, I take credit for that. As I am sure you could imagine I am not the only one to have his body die whilst in this reality, though we are few. Those like The Bastard fear us, for it is us who exist to halt them and save lives, and will take the opportunity to destroy us when they can. They also worry about our contact with those that can influence against their physical being, for there are some in the real world that we can communicate with, and can use to help.

"So this will be the sixth night since you were side-shifted? That is not good."

Hearing this causes me to abandon all other thoughts; all other questions are cast aside. I hope I have misheard, but with no other noise besides the sound of his voice, I know exactly what Hasad has just said and his words cause a tightening in my stomach. I need to know more, but I am too scared to ask any questions for I fear the answers. My mouth opens and closes several times before I can finally put

a voice to my worries. "Wh-what do you mean 'not good'?"

"I assume you know of SIDS, or Sudden Infant Death Syndrome? Cot death?"

The question causes an even stronger tightening in my stomach, steel bands crimping closed. By nature I am a pessimistic person and will look for the worst of things. With the failure of so many early pregnancies, after Lucas's safe and healthy arrival into the world, my mind, the evil thing that it is, turned to the terrible maladies that can befall a young child, the primary fear that of cot death. That fear was diminishing as he grew bigger and stronger each day, and we got closer to the six month age where the risk of SIDS considerably reduced. To hear the question asked now, con-jures up the worry I had put myself through, the nights of getting up to Lucas to check he was still breathing, sitting in the room with him to make sure. Jenny didn't know all the time I had spent doing that, for I had become obsessed with the thought of it striking Lucas down, hoping that my nightly vigils would prevent it from taking my son.

I am unsure as to why Hasad has asked me this, and fear asking for clarity. But I am here to find answers.

"Yes, I know it all too well. I worried constantly that we'd lose our son to it, but now that he's cleared five months and is getting closer to six, I'm hopeful he's passed the main risk." I pause, nervous to ask the question that I have to ask, a fear of the answer already spreading through my body as though a spider's egg has let loose the dozens of spiders contained within. "Why do you ask?"

The words leave my mouth and hang in the darkness. Once again I wonder if Hasad has left, as for a time, silence is the only answer. "Hasad, please tell me, tell me something that's not going to..." I trail off, unable to finish, hoping the unspoken is evident enough.

SHADES OF REALITY

"I'm sorry Nigel, but these *things*, whatever they really are, are the cause of cot death. You will wonder why your son is still sleeping one day and go to wake him only to find his life gone. The Bastard is stealing your son's life and will leave you nothing more than the shell when he's done."

Chapter 10

I sit stone still for a few seconds as I am forced to digest his words, my body numb, before the paralysis breaks and a rush of energy fills my body. I shoot to my feet, legs feeling like rubber as they struggle to support my weight. My hands form fists of rage as a vision of Lucas's funereal marches through my mind. I release an unintelligible cry of despair, the anguish that has flooded my body needing to be set free. I turn towards the vicinity of the door through which I entered and run, my legs shaking underneath me. The anger I feel is greater than anything I have ever known. I have only one thing on my mind, to get back home and destroy The Bastard. I have no idea how to do it, but the rage blinds me to that, my focus on the result, not the means.

The sensation of running through the darkness towards a wall causes me no concern. Before I know it, I've emerged from the building's darkness and am back outside, the minimal light giving me visibility, but nothing stops my pace as I look around to catch my bearings, to confirm where my egress has left me. In doing so, I immediately enter another building, once again passing through the wall as though it isn't there.

The rage that propelled me into moving suddenly washes away, going as fast as it filled me, leaving me with an ache throughout my body, and a brief emptiness before despair fills the void. There is no worse feeling than what I have now, knowing your child is going to die and there is nothing that can be done to save him. For a parent to even think about having to bury their child—their only child—is too much to contemplate. I slow my running and fall to my

knees, totally deflated, and hold my hands to my head, wishing I had hair long enough to grasp and pull. I squeeze my eyes shut, only now realising tears are falling from them, and curse at the unfairness of this. The deep ache I feel worsens when the image of a small coffin in a crowded chapel floats across my mind's eye. I struggle to retain a grip on things, for Lucas's death hasn't occurred, and wallowing here is no way to prevent it from happening. I feel the need to keep crying, but there are more important things to do.

I wipe my eyes and lower my hands looking at my surroundings. I am in a storage area with boxes and pallets stacked everywhere. I see names like Sony, Sanyo, Panasonic. I want to take the boxes and throw them to the ground, using destruction to rid my body of the despair and other tumultuous feelings. But I know I cannot touch them, let alone cause damage. "Shit," I mutter to myself. "Shit, goddamn shit."

It then dawns on me that in my blind rage all I've done is waste time and possibly lose my connection to the only person I can use to help me. I berate myself—silently hating the way I feel. But I know I need to shake myself from this stupor for I cannot help Lucas kneeling here, no matter how much physical and emotional pain I feel. I get to my feet and decide to go back out the way I came; I'll have more perspective of where I am from outside than from standing inside a warehouse.

I turn and come face to face with a shadowy figure.

Chapter 11

I jump back before recognising the face of Hasad. "Easy now. You have to calm down," he tells me. "We can help you, but you and I need to discuss things first."

"I'm sorry." I hold my hands up to him, and see them shaking. This sign of weakness scares me, so I let them drop from sight. "Your words, they made me angry at this thing. And at me, for leaving this so long and allowing it to continue hurting my son. I need your help. We have to save my son. Please, whatever it takes." I look him in the eyes, using the weak light coming from the electric globes above to really see him. "Please help me, and tell me what I need to know."

I swipe at my leaking eyes again and see Hasad nod his head. Before he can add anything, a rattling noise comes from behind me. I turn and see a door slide open allowing extra light into the storage area. Silhouetted in the doorway is a dark figure backlit by the store's lighting. It moves into the relative darkness of the area we inhabit, coming straight for us. I cannot make out any features, but wonder if The Bastard has, after all, come out to hunt me down. Although the figure looks taller and much thinner than my own body, I stand stone still and watch as it gets closer, wondering if the change of body shape is a trick of the lighting.

Hasad taps me on the shoulder and I jump in fright, but turn to look at him. "Just a worker, probably a security guard. We've got other things to worry about. Come on." He returns his left hand to my shoulder and gives it a reassuring squeeze.

"Your action was understandable. To hear of the

potential harm to your child, well, you would be more a monster than The Bastard if rage did not overcome you. Of course I'll help you. But there is more we need to discuss and then we will plan. Let's go."

Hasad turns, and walks back the way we came. I take one last glance over my shoulder to assure myself I face no harm from the dark figure, and see that he is not someone I need to fear.

I am led from the building back into the alley. But rather than re-enter that place, Hasad walks away from it. I jog up to him, keeping silent pace as he looks for the place to start the next phase of our conversation. Fear and rage both still boil inside me, as well as defeat, but I try to swallow the poisonous concoction down. I desperately want to stop Hasad and shake answers from him, but I use everything in my power to prevent myself from doing that. I just hope that a few more minutes will not be the difference between being a parent or being a father grieving his lost child.

"My delivery was probably not the best, and I apologise," he tells me, "but when you spend so much time alone, you forget how to interact with others." We continue to walk back the way we originally came, the background noise increasing as we make our way closer to people and the traffic on the roads, though at this late hour there is considerably less of each.

"Whatever The Bastard is, and I hope to find out one day, he is slowly stealing something from your son that will eventually cause your boy's death. It is this mysterious death that has become known as Sudden Infant Death Syndrome. I know the creatures cause the death, but what the children actually die of, I just don't know. Perhaps it is the soul or life force that is stolen, providing sustenance for the creatures.

Or it could be merely for fun, having no nourishable benefit to them. Whatever it is, the result is the same."

His words fan the fires of the rage I am containing. There is an immense hatred against this creature and what it plans to do against—what it is already doing to!—my family. As difficult as it is to do, I have to put the rage aside and focus on Hasad and what he can do to help. We have now emerged fully from the back alleyways and stand alongside Crocs Road. A scattering of cars drive by in both directions, loud thumping music from one. There is no longer any foot traffic on either side of the road, the last couple entering their car parked slightly down the road from us, the passenger very unsteady on his drunken legs. For the moment we are safe from the searing pain of contact.

"One day you will find your boy dead. You will have no idea of what has happened, retaining the memories of the inhabitant's time in your body as if you have lived those days as you normally do. Only your child's life has been cruelly taken from you."

The words are not new—he has repeated the same awful facts—but when the word "dead" is said aloud, I flinch and feel my hands tighten into fists once more.

"I need to stop him, Hasad." I look to the other man and reach both my hands out to grasp his upper arms, and squeeze them, hard. "I cannot imagine the hurt and pain you have lived through, but I have had my own pain, and losing my son is more than I'll be able to take. What can I do? What can *we* do?"

His face is filled with a pained expression. He has his own pain, its etchings clearly visible, and it is this that reassures me he is an ally and has told me nothing but the truth. I tell myself it is the *other* that is my enemy, not this tortured soul before me.

"I have helped many, and am here to help you. But it is not easy. As with the story of the attack on my family, the only way to save your son is to make The Bastard want to leave your body before it has finished stealing from your boy. They will abandon the child's force to avoid death. But to swap out from your body, they must have you, in the form you take now, close by. If you are not close, the transfer will not happen and your body will die, leaving you like me, to be forever stuck, a part of both worlds, but at home in neither."

I relax my fingers and let go of Hasad's arms, letting my own drop to my side and hang limp, shoulders slumped. His plan sounds easy, but I have no idea how I can execute this. My gaze travels into the distance as I ponder my options. I need to make The Bastard fear that my body is in enough danger that he will forego whatever he's stealing from Lucas. But I have not been able to make an impact on him myself, and I cannot interact with anyone in the real world, so what can I do? Frustration tenses my body.

I turn my attention back to Hasad and ask the obvious question. "How can we do it? It seems I cannot affect him at all, that he is like steel and I am merely a shadow against him. And I cannot interact with the people around me. All attempts to do so end in pain, and they can never see or hear my words." My anger is mounting and my voice rises several levels towards the end.

Hasad shakes his head a little. "I cannot tell you how we will do it, for there is no set way. But despite your experience, there are people that can help, and one of these will play a role; I will make contact with one once I leave you. But any more than that, I cannot yet say. We will find a manner that puts your body in danger and makes him feel compelled to vacate it. But you must also consider the risk to

yourself, for to make The Bastard fearful enough, your body may actually be in danger, and this plan may not work the way we hope. Are you prepared for that risk?"

I don't need to think to answer. I am flooded with memories and images of Lucas, those of events that have been, and those that are many years into his future that I have already thought and dreamed about. I would hope my loss would be painful for Jenny, but I know the loss of Lucas, to Jenny and me, would be far worse. "Of course I am prepared to take the risk. But how and who can you use to help? How can we make that happen, real or not?"

"Oh it will need to be real. If it is not, The Bastard will recognize the trap and the chance will be lost." He has not answered my question of who will help, but he starts to walk again and indicates that I should follow, which I do, stepping alongside and matching his stride. I want to push the point and scrub away all doubt, but he hasn't finished talking yet. "If you are able to keep him thinking that you have not left the house and therefore have no additional knowledge, he may be less suspicious of any subsequent actions."

Hasad stops walking and puts his hand on my chest to stop my movement. "Where do you live Nigel? It must be getting early now so we should head towards your home. We can talk on the way and work out details, formulate a plan that will return you to your body before it's too late to save your child."

Chapter 12

I arrive back home having left Hasad twenty minutes earlier, a rough plan laid out. Hasad didn't want to get too close to the house for fear of The Bastard sensing his presence. If that happened, it could lose me the slim advantage I may hold on The Bastard not knowing the two of us had met.

Rather than go directly into the house, I enter the garage first. If The Bastard is awake and has noticed me missing, hopefully he has not checked the garage and I'll be able to convince him that I've been out here. Of course if he is up I'll be hard pressed to maintain the lie of having not left the house at all. Concern tingles its way up my spine, knowing that the time has arrived.

Preparing myself for the potential onslaught to come, I walk through the connecting door into the house. I listen intently for any noise that would betray someone moving around, but the house seems quiet, silence only broken by the gurgle of the refrigerator. I'm not clear yet though, since I don't know if The Bastard has been up at all during the night to look for me. This will only be confirmed when we confront each other for the first time today.

I look up as I make my way from the entryway through to the living area and notice a faint glow coming from there. I mentally run through my story of being in the garage, but add the element of going to sit out front for a short period, to shake off the claustrophobia of being locked in the house for several days. As I close the distance to the living room, and the glow brightens, I start to doubt my ability to pull off both the story of my whereabouts tonight, and the lies I will need to tell to enact the vague plan Hasad had crafted during

our walk from the city.

I emerge from the darkened hallway, expecting The Bastard to immediately question me, shattering any chance of maintaining my cover story. Though there is a person sitting in the chair, it is not The Bastard, but Jenny. She's reading a Disc World novel, one she has probably read at least three or four times already. I start to ask her why she's up so early (I sneak a look at the clock on the wall above her and see it's 5:50am), but halt before voicing anything, for she isn't going to hear me.

Instead I move closer to her and reach my hand out, a pang of loss striking me, not for the first time during this ordeal. I realise how much I miss being able to talk to her, hold her and just spend time knowing that we are together. I console myself however with a hope that it will be over soon and we'll be back together (although I know that if things go wrong, I will never get closer to her than I am right now...but I hastily push these thoughts aside for I need to remain focussed and confident). Just the thought of holding her again is enough to spur me on and make sure I fortify my resolve to reel The Bastard into a trap that will end his control over—and slow destruction of—my family.

I leave Jen to her reading, figuring she must have just been in to see Lucas and decided it wasn't worth going back to bed. Not the first time either of us has made that decision, leaving the other to get some extra sleep.

I walk down to Lucas's room and sit on the floor near the cot. I hope that being in the same room as him will help provide me with the calming environment I need to make sure I am ready for the first meeting of the day with The Bastard.

I sit in silence and replay the conversations with Hasad, locking in tight what was discussed, and working out how to

best make the play. I figure I'll only have one shot and if I blow it, I have no way of getting in contact with Hasad to work out a change of plan. With this realisation I feel pressure mounting, and a fear of getting it wrong which causes a sickening feeling in the pit of my stomach. But I don't want these negative thoughts; I don't want the risk of them swaying my attitude and how I handle myself, especially when I need to be at my strongest.

*   *   *

Dawn is breaking outside, light filtering around the blinds, and I can see the outline of Lucas, lying motionless as he sleeps. Everything I am doing I will be doing for him, to save him—

The Bastard is stealing your son's life and will leave you nothing more than the shell when he's done. Hasad's words from earlier echo through my mind. I have a sudden feeling—the worst thing I have ever felt—that we're too late.

I burst to my feet, panic and a red hot rage flooding my body once again, grief intermingling with it. I lean close to Lucas, my body slipping through his cot, and use my hand to try to rock him awake. My hand of course passes through him, the flaring pain barely felt within the jumble that my mind has become. An ache of loss burns the back of my throat.

I clench my fists and look up, looking through my son's bedroom wall right to where I know my sleeping body lies. I take two steps in that direction before Hasad's words, different ones, come to my mind, stopping me. *You will wonder why your son is still sleeping one day and go to wake him only to find his life gone.* If Lucas is dead (the thought of the word associated with him terrifies me, ice cubes slipping

69

down my back), then I should have been pulled back to my body, The Bastard gone to wherever he exists between the stealing of innocent lives.

Confusion washes over me. If I am still out of my body and aware of the things that have occurred over the past week, then The Bastard cannot be done, my son's life not yet stolen. I rush back to the cot, kneel down and place my ear as close to Lucas's mouth as I can, taking advantage of my movement through physical objects. Whilst I cannot feel anything in this form, I hear faint breaths—inhale, exhale.

"Oh thank God," I whisper. Leaning back from the cot, I drop to the floor and sit, holding my head in my hands as I shake it to and fro, my whole body trembling from the rush of emotions. I stay that way until Lucas wakes from his sleep and lets out his "come and get me" cry some unknown time later.

The sudden noise breaks me from the fugue I have fallen into, giving me the last bit of reassurance I need that Lucas is okay and there is still time to end this in his favour.

I stand, and walk towards the door, only to have it open just before I get there and my own body stride through. I move aside from The Bastard who glances my way briefly, but says nothing.

"Morning," I say, trying to cast an element of cheer to my voice, when what I really want to do is beat his head against the wall until the body falls lifeless to the floor. This *thing's* intention to steal the life from my son is all that swirls through my mind, pure hatred waiting on the periphery to join the mix. But I swallow it down, a bitter taste that burns my throat and stomach.

From the hallway I hear Jenny coming, alerted to the cries of our child. "Is my little man awake again?" She walks into the room as The Bastard pulls Lucas from the cot.

"There he is. Come to mummy."

With what I detect as some regret, The Bastard hands Lucas to Jenny, giving her a good morning kiss in the process. I figure he is disappointed that she made her way to the room so quickly, stealing his opportunity to suck some more of the life from Lucas. This gives me a jolt of satisfaction and a little more confidence that it's not too late to save my son.

Chapter 13

During our walk from the city, Hasad had vaguely outlined the plan and allowed me to fill in the blanks based on what would work best for me, what would raise the least suspicion with The Bastard. It was agreed to keep it simple to avoid the need for me to create a complex lie that would only increase the possibility of getting it wrong. Lucas's life is reliant on this going right. I have to succeed.

The plan seemed simple: get The Bastard to follow me out of the house, using whatever pretence possible. In my mind I hope that his insistence last night in keeping me in the house can be used. If I try to leave and he is against it, I will reason with him that he should come with me. It is not uncommon for me to do that, giving both Jen a break, but also giving me some time alone with the little one. A full time job limits my time with him, while Jenny has all day every day. He was already very clingy to her, which I could understand; she was his source of food, was there every time he woke and was the primary care giver when he needed the attention. I was gone most days and spent less than two hours with him in the evenings before he'd be put to bed, and barely an hour of a morning before heading off to work. But this whole experience has me focussed on making sure that work, whilst essential, will never come between my son and me, and the time and attention he deserves from his dad.

Once outside, I will lead The Bastard to the local park. Hasad and I visited it briefly last night as part of our planning. I suggested the park since it would be a place that should raise no suspicion with The Bastard; a common place for Lucas and I to go, of which The Bastard will know from

my memories.

Once we arrive at the park, *something* will happen. Hasad refused to tell me what, saying that he wanted me to be surprised, to reduce any arousal of suspicion in The Bastard. His reasoning was that if I showed no surprise when the time came, The Bastard would see the setup. I insisted that Hasad tell me, not admitting why. I mistrusted The Bastard's intentions, when along came Hasad, providing me with explanations that I believed...but was it only because I *wanted* to believe them? *Needed* to? Were they true? When talking to Hasad and hearing his story I had no doubt at the time it was true, but I was vulnerable and needed an ally. His words painted him as that ally so I believed what I was told. But as we walked back towards home I started to doubt; the pessimist in me wondering if I was easy pickings and if in fact maybe The Bastard knew I'd leave the house and had somehow set me up with Hasad. After all, I had seen little difference between the two so perhaps they were working together. Or Hasad was an evil unto himself, not at all affiliated with The Bastard, but some*thing* else after the same prize that was my son. Or maybe I was his target. The potentials were endless.

Despite my insistence, Hasad would not relent, only offering me a hint of what was to come. *I don't yet know what will be done, Nigel,* he had said. *I have ideas that I will work on and someone I will meet with that will help. Things will be ready by 11am. So just follow what we discussed, and make sure he is there. We will win this, and you will have your family back.*

His words were convincing, although his tone wasn't. That had ended it, but the doubt circled, only until the resignation settled in—the realisation that I could do nothing anyway. I resolved that if at anytime I detected anything that

looked like it would harm Lucas, I would find a way to protect him, heedless of any cost to myself.

Eventually Hasad and I parted, both leaving the park at the same time but in different directions. I convinced myself to believe and trust in Hasad more than I would trust The Bastard. And if that trust was misguided then I would find a way to end the suffering it would cause me through the loss of my son.

*   *   *

It has been an hour or more since Lucas woke and I have been doing what I can to avoid The Bastard, or to at least limit the opportunities for us to interact, by spending time close to Jen. He may have slipped up once by talking to me with her present, but I didn't think he would do that again.

They eat crispy bacon, eggs, and crumpets slathered with butter and jam, following their mouthfuls of food with hot coffee. Even though I do not feel hunger, missing out on this breakfast, my favourite of the week, gives me phantom hunger pangs. I love Friday mornings, or at least I used to, my working week finished, meaning I can lounge at the dining table a little longer than on a work day, reading more of the paper than just the funnies. Although I can't smell it, I know the odour of coffee and bacon will linger on the air, a reminder of the breakfast that had been. On the floor in his bouncinette is Lucas, cooing at the jungle animals attached to it, moving around enough to make them dance, and bring a sad smile to my face.

While they eat, I sit at the window in the living room, looking outside, allowing their voices from the dining room to fade into background noise. The sun is shining, the trees gently moving in the morning breeze. The occasional car

drives by, momentarily breaking the serenity I find by just sitting and staring.

Inside my mind and body is anything but serene. As the second hand clicks its way around the clock's face minute after minute, sounding as loud as a gunshot each time, I know that I am running out of time. I won't be able to procrastinate much longer but will need to set the wheels in motion for what I hope will be a success (*know*, my mind screams, what I *know* will be a success). But still, no matter how much I want—*need*—to believe Hasad, the lingering doubt eats at me. Instead of walking The Bastard into a trap, the trap could be for me. Or worse still, Lucas.

"I'm nearly done here." The words break me of my ruminations, but I pay no attention to them thinking it a conversation between the happy couple. Then, still looking out the window and dreading what needs to be done, I feel a hand on my shoulder, an almost gentle caress. I flinch in response and turn to look at the owner of the hand.

I look up into my own face, so close it causes fear and hatred to clench my stomach in their two-fisted grip. The fingers tighten on my shoulder. "I'm almost done here," he says, and I realise the words had been for me.

"I—I'm glad to hear that," I stammer in reply, fear's grip on my stomach tightening more than the hand on my shoulder. I look back out the window for I cannot look at the face and hope to keep the anger from visibly crossing my own. If he is nearly done, my little boy is near death (*if Hasad is to be believed*, my mind reminds me). With that realisation I struggle to contain the rage that wants to erupt from me in swinging fists and kicking feet. "I hope that, um, that my son has been helpful to you." I don't care to hear an answer or to even talk to this thing, but I need to. I think back to my dealings with him over the last few days and

remind myself that I need to continue in the same way, for I need The Bastard to think that today is no different from yesterday; that I know no more than I did last night when he went to bed.

"It has been good for the both of us. But tell me, what did you do last night? Did the urge to leave the house overcome my advice?"

I am glad I'm still looking out the window, for his words strike me like a fist to the solar plexus, and I feel a pained expression cross my face. Does he know I left the house and is testing me, wanting to see if I lie? The voice gave no hint of mistrust or doubt. If I answer in a lie and he calls me on it, where will that leave me? But if he doesn't know that I left and I admit I did, how will that lead me through the rest of the morning and what needs to be done? Hasad was clear that if The Bastard felt I had remained house-bound, this would be a big advantage for us. I have to buy some time to think of the right answer, to maintain the, albeit small, advantage.

I slowly get to my feet and turn to face him. It's time to talk, and I don't know what the right thing to say is. "Well, you were pretty adamant that it wasn't wise to leave." His stare is penetrating, as though he is boring into my mind to seek out the truth, and I need to get myself away from it. So while talking, I move away from him towards the wall and the wedding portrait that hangs there, one larger posed picture with several candid shots inlaid around it. "I appreciated your concern but did still consider going out, to give myself a break from feeling trapped."

I don't hear it, but feel The Bastard approach and stand next to me, also gazing at the frozen images of that day so many years ago. "I love this place but never thought I'd spend so much time in it with no interaction with my

family." I finally turn to face him, realising an opportunity to lead into the story to get us both out of the house. "So I spent a good portion of the night outside in the backyard—" I choose to say backyard due to less windows that look out to it, therefore less chance he would have gone looking out there "—just looking at the night sky and thinking about the joy of holding my son again soon." My voice hitches at the last bit, a mixture of true emotion at the craving I feel to hold the little guy and blow raspberries on his tummy, and the fear of this thing stealing that chance, while I stand around and do nothing about it.

The Bastard slowly turns from the photo and looks at me, a softer expression on his face, eyes no longer seeking the truth. "I can't say that—"

His words are cut off as Jenny comes through the doorway, carrying Lucas against her chest, still wearing her dressing gown. "Were you talking to me, sweetheart?"

He is momentarily caught. He turns his back to me and faces Jen. I wish I could pick up a knife or a suitably blunt object to stab or bludgeon him with. I go so far as to look around for something to use, knowing that even if I find one, I won't be able to do anything with it.

"Just talking to myself, reminiscing about our wonderful wedding day." Even though I cannot see his face, I can hear the smile in the voice, a genuine joy at my memories of the wedding. "I thought you were making the bed?"

A huge grin spreads across Jen's face, reaching into her eyes and giving them some added shine. "I decided it wasn't worth making." I watch as her grin grows mischievous. "After your efforts last night my dear, I figure I'd like to take advantage of whatever has spiked your adventurousness and go back for some more tonight." She reaches over and gives the flesh version of my ass a squeeze. I look away from her,

disgust roiling in my stomach. *My wife is more impressed by this foul creature than she is of me! How could this be happening!* I am crushed, my resolve to save Lucas and my family momentarily dimming, my confidence shattered. But it is for a brief moment only, as regardless of the impression made on my wife, the loss of our child is far more tragic.

I turn my head once again taking in the two of them. The smile remains on Jenny's face as she too, now stares at the photo, as though admiring the work of a master artist. "Wasn't it a great day?" she says. "Perfect weather, perfect people. So long ago, but still remember it like it was yesterday." She leans in for a kiss, one that turns very passionate for the briefest of moments and causes me yet another point of hatred against The Bastard, and some sorrow at the potential disappointment I am to my wife.

Stepping back she hands Lucas to The Bastard. "I'm going for my shower, so you're on babysitting duties," she says as my son lets out a cry at being given up by his mother. I like to think it's because Lucas knows there is something different about dad right now, and at least *he* prefers the real one. *Soon,* I think to him, almost verbalising it. *Soon it* will *be daddy holding you again.*

Jenny leaves the room destined for the shower. The Bastard briefly looks my way and then, with a huge smile spreading over his face, turns after Jen. "If you want another go with the tiger, why don't I come on down and join you in the shower? Would hate to keep you waiting until tonight."

"You dirty bastard!" Insanity washes over me and I lunge at him. I vaguely hear Jen's raucous laugh, followed by words that I don't even try to interpret through the red mist that has overcome me. With my hands at his throat, The Bastard turns to me, and with Lucas now in one arm, uses his right to shove me aside, sending me crashing to the floor.

SHADES OF REALITY

His face still wears a smile as he quietly says, "Seems the wife likes what she got last night. I just hope you had as much fun as we did."

Lying on the floor and looking up at him, I want to launch into a barrage of curses and insults, for the little good they will do. Instead I continue to stare, trying to will this thing into a painful death, and feel the scowl on my face.

As though ignoring the entire incident, his free right arm extends towards me, offering me assistance in getting up. I don't take it, but stand on my own, keeping my eyes locked on his, trying to show him my lack of fear. Amongst the hatred in the room, there is still innocence when Lucas farts loudly. I'd normally find this funny, but today, it is just another reminder of what is at stake. The Bastard however finds it amusing and laughs quietly, moving Lucas to a two arm hold, and rocks him gently, looking down at him with a caring look. I wonder if the look is anything more than someone viewing a tasty morsel.

Neutrality returns to his face as the brown eyes return to me. "Now before that meddling woman walked in and interrupted me, as good as the interruption was, I was telling you that I'm not overly impressed that you *risked* yourself by going outside when I advised against it." There is emphasis added to his use of 'risked,' a snide undertone, almost a taunt, that makes me continue to boil inside. This along with the recent events turns my complete trust to Hasad, a final decision made as to whom I need to align to, putting an end to the internal struggle as to who is telling the truth, and wondering from where the biggest risk lay.

I bite back the desire to scream at him and instead, using a calm voice say, "I respected your advice, and appreciate it, which is why I didn't venture further than the backyard. I figured if I had a problem, I'd be back inside in

no time." I don't know where the words have come from, but I am happy with the way I have responded despite the many emotions I have in my mind. I then look him square in the eyes to show the truth (or so I hope) of my words. Whereas my mind is running the race of fear, I feel a confidence that I hope he can detect.

"Next time you want a walk, which there probably won't be since I think I'll be done tomorrow, let me know and I'll escort you. Your protector, if you will."

Hearing these words I want to hug this hated thing, for the opportunity I need to get us out of the house has just been presented on a platter. Silver even.

Containing the elation I feel at how easy this has become, I stare at The Bastard and ask, "So how about today then? Maybe later this morning we can take Lucas for a walk down to the park." Now that I have my trust firmly aligned to Hasad, I have less concern about trying to keep Lucas away from whatever may be planned for later this morning. To get The Bastard from the house and to the park without Lucas would be a tall order, so I have opted to go for the path with the least complication. Only a very small part of my mind admonishes me for making this decision, not out of distrust for Hasad, but a lack of true knowledge as to what I will be walking us into, and what danger there may be for Lucas.

I watch closely for a reaction, but see nothing, so I continue, enjoying the momentum I feel building. "Last night outside felt great, and when I came back inside I felt claustrophobic, which sounds silly, I know. But I'd really like to head out for a walk.

"It isn't unusual for Lucas and I to have some father and son time, so Jen will be fine with it." I halt here as The Bastard distracts me by doing what I have seen him do many

times already, but has a much greater impact now. He has lifted Lucas to his face (Lucas having drifted to sleep, I notice) and placed his mouth over the bottom half of Lucas's face, his eyes on me the whole time, as though taunting me. I try to ignore his actions, to show I am not concerned by this, but a tickle reaches the back of my mind. *He said he'll be gone tomorrow...what if this is the last time he needs to steal from Lucas and after this, Lucas will be lost the next time he sleeps?*

"Stop it!" I yell and move at The Bastard. For whatever reason—the tone of my voice hinting at something, or just plain amusement at my outburst—he lowers Lucas from his mouth, a string of saliva linking the two until distance breaks it. There is an element of amusement on The Bastard's face. He looks at my hands, both of which are balled into fists, and laughs, a laugh that seeps with malice and contempt; so much so that had I heard that laugh anytime before, I would have spent all of this last week trying to find a way to destroy this thing.

"What's the matter little man? Don't like what I'm doing to your son? Prefer what I did to your wife, do you?" The malice and contempt from his laugh carries through to his voice, a voice that now only partly resembles my own. There is a cold look of hatred welling up into his eyes, and I am sure I see a momentary darkening of the sclera, as though something passed behind it. I take an involuntary step back (just as Lucas emits a little mewl and wakes up), but the passive face is once again on display, its true form in hiding. I fear that my haste to stop him may have revealed that I know more than I am supposed to. Quickly looking away from my own body I search for the words to say that will back me out of this. But I am freed of the need when The Bastard starts talking in my normal voice, rocking Lucas in

his arms to prevent the crying that is on the cusp of happening.

"I can imagine how seeing that must make you feel, but as you've been told, there is no harm being done. Relax."

You lying sonofabitch! The fear that he has taken his last fill from my child sickens me. But I knock it down, keep it at bay for the moment with the hope that having just stopped him means he has not yet finished, and I still have a hope of this turning out right. Plus, I'm still standing staring at myself which means I haven't returned to my body, a sure sign he hasn't completed his task. I hope.

"Th-thanks." The worry and nerves I feel come through in the one stuttered word. I again look at him, but can see no evidence of the earlier glance I got of the true feelings this thing has for me and my family. I wonder for the first time, why he feels the need to put on this charade if he is truly as invincible as he has proven to be; with no way of directly harming him myself and no way I can interact with anyone around me—although Hasad indicated otherwise. Why not taunt me with the fact that he is tearing my family apart? Is his worry that knowledge like that would drive a person out to the street where he might find someone like Hasad?

Keeping my eyes on The Bastard and not wanting to allow any more face sucking to occur, I return to the conversation prior to the distraction. "So how about that walk? Looks like a nice enough day outside." I use my hand to gesture at the window, golden sunshine streaming in through the open curtain. "Probably still cold out, but that certainly won't bother me." I chuckle hoping to break the tension that I feel has built between the two of us. The Bastard shows no response to my attempt at lightening the moment, but continues to stare at me, face stoic.

After a few more tense moments, my spirits are lifted

when, after looking out the window, The Bastard nods his head. Looking down at Lucas he responds to him. "How about daddy takes you out for a walk?"

The agreement to take the walk has come easier than I expected. He then looks up at me. "I'll go let the wife know we're going out." With Lucas to his chest he turns and heads towards the back of the house and our bedroom, where Jenny is using the shower.

Relief and joy flood through my body, as though a wall damming them has been knocked down. Floating in the joy are elements of doubt and concern, but I have to cast them aside and move ahead with the plan, as loose as it is.

I walk through to the kitchen, needing to keep moving as a sense of adrenaline kicks in, creating a nervous energy. I can hear the shower running and the low muffle of unintelligible voices, and try not to ponder on The Bastard being with my naked wife. I move through the kitchen and look at the dirty dishes in the sink, waiting to be loaded into the dishwasher. I glance behind me at the bench top, my eyes falling to the microwave. Its green numerals tell me it is 9:46. I turn away paying this no mind but suddenly stop. *Things will be ready by 11am.* The words of Hasad strike through my mind like a church bell ringing. If we go now, we'll be almost an hour early!

All joy and relief of things having fallen into place shatter around me. I feel a sinking feeling that is all the more painful because it comes so soon after a high. I walk to the TV unit and look at the clock on the video, hoping that it is later than what the microwave has told me. Its electronic glow adds to the conspiracy: 9:47. I curse to myself. How can I stall for another hour? How can I have been so stupid not to think of the time earlier when The Bastard agreed to leave the house and tried to immediately stall? If I interject now it

will surely raise a hint of doubt that could crush all hope.

I hear The Bastard's voice more clearly; he is on his way back to the kitchen. I am still by the TV unit, no idea as to what I'm going to be able to do. I briefly consider using the excuse we should bring Jenny along to allow me to spend more time with her as well as Lucas, but not knowing what is planned or will happen, I don't want to risk having her with us. If my body is put in harm of death, then she will surely interject in some way which will either put her at risk, or have the plan unfold around me. Having Lucas with me still leaves me with some dread, but I hope with him in the pram, he'll be safe. But Jen...without knowing details of Hasad's plan, I'm not willing to take the risk of her possible interference.

The Bastard makes his entrance from the hallway, still talking. I turn and see that he has been talking to Lucas who is now bundled in a jacket and little blue beanie—what Jen and I refer to as his 'thug cap' as it gives him the appearance of a little, albeit very cute and harmless, thug. The Bastard himself is now dressed, gone is the light grey tracksuit, replaced with a pair of blue jeans and black turtleneck jumper.

"Off we go to the sunshine and fresh air." I get the feeling The Bastard is as much talking to me as Lucas. I am at a cross roads now: speak up and try to delay our departure or agree to go, and risk the consequences of being early.

Chapter 14

The Bastard walks right past me and heads towards the front of the house. I stare as he passes, frozen, not able to interject and try to halt him, but feeling the need to.

"Shouldn't we...or you...help Jen out and load the dishwasher? Might be nice for her if that's done." I am looking back over my shoulder towards the sink, hoping that I can get back a few minutes. I feel that every second I can delay our leaving may have large returns. When I turn back to The Bastard, he's shaking his head.

"I don't get you. You moan about wanting to go out, and now you want the dishes put away? They normally stay in the sink until after lunch, so what's the big deal?"

The stalling tactic has failed. With resignation I say, "Just thought it would have been nice," and, giving up that approach, head towards the entranceway from where he is still staring at me. If I cannot arrange for us to leave later, I'll have to do as much as I can to stall on the way to the park, to have us there as close to 11am as I can manage. Everything else is out of my hands, and I feel the burden of that dragging my spirits down.

Lucas is left on the floor while The Bastard puts his shoes on. Lucas lies there and moves his arms and legs, looking somewhat like a turtle not able to right itself. He isn't yet rolling from his back to his front, but I figure that will be the next milestone for Jen and I to witness...if we don't lose him first.

The ache of sorrow that thought causes makes me pause, and not for the first time, I want to fall to the ground and cry. But I find strength; a strength born from necessity, and

stay on my feet, tears held back.

"Jen was okay with you..." I start to ask.

The Bastard pauses briefly in doing up his left shoe and glares at me. "Why wouldn't she be?"

I raise my hands in a placating gesture. "Sorry. Sheesh."

He goes back to his shoes and I look down at my own feet, still wearing cheap slippers that I cannot get rid of. Lucas gurgles in some form of amusement as The Bastard, finished with his shoes, picks him up from the floor. Ignoring my apology, he opens the interior door to the garage, steps out, and closes it behind him, its thud like the closing of a coffin lid.

Please Hasad, please...you have to have things ready. With an outward sigh, I move forward and step through the closed door.

I see that Lucas has been strapped into his pram and has grabbed his LaMaze dog that hangs from the top of it. He playfully swats it, happy gurgles accompanying his movements.

"So, to the park then?" I ask, making sure that this is still the destination. And if it isn't I'll need to quickly find a way to make it.

"Sure, why not," he replies. "My lovely wife was so happy with the news of us going for a walk to the park she said she may meet us down there."

His words derail my thoughts. Not knowing of Hasad's plan I cannot say whether Jenny's presence will place her in danger, or jeopardise whatever plan has been concocted. I'd rather her not be anywhere nearby, but since I cannot *risk* trying to get The Bastard to prevent it, I have to let the worry go.

The Bastard presses the button to open the garage door. Sunlight streams through the ever increasing gap as the door

slowly lifts up. I imagine the warmth of the sun as the light reaches me, but it doesn't even cause my shadow to be cast behind me.

"Let's go," The Bastard says to Lucas as he starts to push the pram. He rolls out through the garage door and hits the remote we have attached to the pram, the door once again rumbling to life, this time closing, stealing the bright light away from the garage and inviting the darkness back to rule. After a brief moment, I follow.

To get to the park we have to go down along the creek, following a bike path, and then cross over a footbridge and walk a short distance more before reaching it. I always go along the creek as it is much quicker than following the road, but also gets us away from traffic and the pollutants they release. There is invariably a lot of bird life along the creek, either swooshing from the sky to snap up a morsel of food from the flowing water, or sitting in the weeping willows that line the creek's bank, their branches hanging down to the ground, like a living curtain. But if I were to encourage him to take the route via the streets, then that would add maybe fifteen minutes to the journey, making it that much closer to 11am when we arrive.

I think about suggesting this, but realise it is already too late as The Bastard, who has moved a distance ahead of me, has already turned left at the end of the drive, and is heading in the direction of the creek. Feeling failure again, I hurry my pace to catch up, but then decide to remain a few paces behind.

After a few minutes of silence between us, but cheerful noises from Lucas, The Bastard turns off the footpath to the bike path that initially slopes down from the road's elevation to the creek's edge. Now that we are away from the few people already on the go, I know I need to find an

opportunity to stall our progress, so I accelerate my speed to catch him.

Moving into stride next to him, Lucas is still full of noise, grunting and gurgling, doing his best impersonation of communication. Overhead there is the screech of a bird in flight, and to my right, the gentle burbling of the water as it flows slowly, but steadily towards the river that will eventually take it out to the ocean. Not seeing anything, but trying to halt our progress, I point between two willows, their hanging branches gently swaying in the breeze, and ask "What was that?"

Whether out of curiosity or an actual interest The Bastard stops and turns to follow my hand. "I'm sure I just saw a fish jump from the water," I add. "Turn the pram around and we'll see if it happens again. Lucas may want to see it." I don't believe a five month old would have any interest, but if it stalls for time, then I'm happy to run with it. The Bastard can think I'm a fool, I don't care.

To my surprise, he seems interested in playing the dad role, and follows my instructions, even to the point of bending down and pointing to the same spot as me and asking Lucas if he can see anything. I smile to myself, but only briefly for we may have stopped for the moment, but when nothing shows itself I'll still be close to an hour ahead of the agreed time.

After a few moments of silence, The Bastard stands and looks at me. "Well, if you saw something, it's gone now. Let's get moving." With that he grabs the pram's handle and sets off at a faster pace than before.

As we round a bend, where the path closes in on the creek, and a large willow partly overhangs both creek and path, a piercing scream fills the air. I immediately look to the sky expecting to see birds flying over, perhaps fighting whilst

in flight. Nothing breaks the clear blue sky save for a few wispy, unshaped clouds moving lazily along.

I turn my attention to The Bastard who is looking over my shoulder, eyes wide and mouth hanging open. I turn towards where I now know the source of the screaming to be. A tall, overweight woman wearing a long dark skirt is running at me, her long, dark hair flapping behind her from beneath a woollen beanie pulled low on her head. This is all I see before she crashes *through* me.

I instinctively put my hands up to protect myself. As she enters the space my body takes I see a knife in her left hand, its long steel blade edged with serrations. Her fingers are gripped tightly around its handle. The sight of this outweighs the searing pain tracking her path through my body.

I turn. She continues to scream, but there is now a cry of fright from The Bastard. Her hand lunges towards him in a left hook motion, and connects with his forehead, above the right eye, but it is not the blade that has hit him. She has clubbed him with the portion of the knife's handle that protrudes from the back of her hand, fingers whitened from her tight grip on it.

The force knocks The Bastard over. As he goes down I see his left hand is caught over the pram's handle, which causes the pram to tip and then topple over, crashing to the asphalt, his head hitting the ground shortly after in a sickening blow. Over the screams of the lady I hear Lucas's cry. I immediately forget all about the attacker and my body, the danger of her and the knife insignificant to the thought that Lucas may be hurt.

I run to the pram and grab for the handle, intending on righting it and calming Lucas. But my hands pass right through as if it isn't there, though it is me who isn't here.

Lucas is still strapped in and crying harder now, a little voice with power like a wailing siren. Unable to do anything for him I turn back to the attacker. Through natural instinct and reaction I let voice a yell for help. The Bastard is making no noise whatsoever; he lays with his stomach to the ground, motionless. He looks as though the blow his head took on the ground has dazed him, or that he has gone into shock. I continue my yelling, though whilst loud in my ears, it carries nothing, not even registering to the attacker that someone else is here. To her, and the rest of the world, I don't exist. To these events I am little more than a viewer, unable to interact or impact on the result.

Realising there is only futility in yelling I stop, and stare at the scene before me. The Bastard is next to the fallen pram, right arm on the ground above his head, the left pinned at his side. The woman who is attacking him—attacking *me!*—sits on his lower back. Her leg has the left arm pinned, but it is the knife in her right hand, which is now pressed into his—*my!*—back, the point having found a gap between the top of the jeans and the black jumper, it having ridden up his back during the fall. I can see blood welling from the wound.

Could this be it? The initial reaction to the attack has passed, and though the fear still grips me, I wonder if this is the setup. That Hasad is behind this. I look around frantically, seeking some sign that will turn that hope into a roaring fire of relief. But I see nothing, save for the swaying branches of the trees, the long grass on the creek's bank stirring. No one, not even a bird in the sky above. No sign of anyone around who has heard the cries of this woman. Or maybe people have heard, but it's not their concern, not something they want to become involved in and potentially become entangled in a web that could snare them, and lead

to their own harm. I know I would likely do the same if faced with distant cries, but for now, I hate people's avoidance of my plight.

Whilst I desperately seek a sign, my hope fades; this feels wrong. Although there were no specific details shared by Hasad, it was supposed to be at the park, and not until 11am. We're probably an hour early, and 10 minutes from the destination. But, I reason, what are the chances of this attack on the same day that *something* was setup to happen?

I fear that Hasad is not responsible for this attack, that I have unwittingly stumbled into someone else's problem.

The attacker is talking nonsense, scaring me with her hysteria. "It was you!" she screams down at The Bastard, who only now is starting to show a sign of lucidity. "You slept with her and told her you loved her, but then you...you didn't want to see her. You abandoned her you pig!" The sun shines on spittle flying from her lips, and I see the knife disappear a little further into the flesh. But still The Bastard makes no sound or movement against the attack. Ever present are the tortured cries of anguish from Lucas. The scene tears at me for I am helpless but to stand and watch. The only one I can have an impact on is the one in danger.

The attacker's screaming and ranting continues. "How could you, you filthy vile *thing*," she spits. "When she realised she would not have you, she felt that life was over." A large sob of anguish escapes between her words, but she bites it back, and continues, her pitch softening to a more intense hatred, while I stand sentinel, no idea what I can do, or if I even need to do anything. "She killed herself. Took tablets and died. You killed her. You bastard! My beautiful sister, my only sister, and you treated her like she was nothing. You are going to pay...you are going to die!"

With the last words her voice rises even further. I am

speechless, for I have no knowledge of what is being said. I have been totally faithful with Jenny since we started dating, and have never acted improperly. I feel guilty even looking at another woman now, let alone thinking thoughts that could lead to any form of relationship, brief or otherwise. The woman must be crazy, and it is this which forms icicles of terror throughout my body, for crazy people will do crazy things, heedless of the impact or consequences.

I suddenly flash to my life before Jen, and my frequent habits of trying to bed women with no intention of anything but some nights of unbridled sex. But it's impossible to think this woman could have held a grudge from something that happened so many years ago. It seems insane to even entertain the thought, but the fear runs deeper still, for there were women in my past that I mistreated.

Despite all this turmoil, I remain still, taking no action, knowing that if I wanted to, I couldn't. I am as active in this as The Bastard; he lies there and does nothing whilst I stand and have the same effect. If this woman sinks the blade deeper and kills my body, I will be stuck in this in-between state as Hasad is. And I would be a witness to the act, forever having to relive my own death. Or if The Bastard swaps out before the killing, there will be nothing of me left. Either way I lose. I need to act. I need to act now.

Knowing it will do me no good but with no other ideas, I lunge at the woman, striking out with fists that could as well be made from marshmallows for the impact they have. With each strike against her I feel the burning in my fists as they sink through my target. I hear the panicked breaths raging in and out of The Bastard as I imagine the uncertainty of the situation overwhelms him.

Giving up with my marshmallow fists I step back and look around for something I can use against her, deep down

knowing there is nothing. I look down at The Bastard; I need to spur him into action. I approach him, ignoring the woman and her cries of hatred and anguish.

"Do something!" I scream into his face, kneeling at his right shoulder, hands grabbing at both of them. "She's crazy. Fight back, goddamnit." I nervously look at her. She continues to accuse me as the reason for her sister's suicide. And even though I cannot believe she is sane or making accurate accusations, a small part of me wonders (and worries) if in reality I have caused this woman's pain in my earlier days of care free attitude, and justified punishment is now being delivered. Guilt briefly sparks, but is extinguished by Lucas's screams, and a reminder of what I have in life now. I may have wronged in the past, but I will not allow those activities to change the life I have now.

The Bastard looks me in the eye, and then turns and briefly stares at the pram, lying on its side, with Lucas screaming from within its confines. There is definitely regret across his face, maybe even despair. His fear is an echo of what I am feeling, a deep etched worry, though for him, I can only presume that it is potentially having been so close to destroying my son, and maybe now, for nothing.

As much as I fear my own body's death, and now feel the alternative is the likely death of my son, I yell at The Bastard again to do something. And then I feel a pull at my entire being, a strange feeling, not one that causes pain, but a pleasant tingling sensation across my skin. But more than the sensation is the thought of what it may mean. *I was pulled back to my body*, Hasad had told me.

As the tug intensifies, I feel an increasing dread that I will be returned to my body only to be killed before I can do something. But I quickly think that if I make it back, I will have control to do something meaningful, and fight my

attacker before she can inflict more harm, and not just allow my body to be defeated as The Bastard has done. As these thoughts are churning my stomach, I hear her whisper words that stop me cold. "Now it is time for you to die."

Before the shudder the words elicit has passed completely through my body, I am distracted by a darkness rising out of the flesh and blood version of my body that lies before me. I scramble away from the prone form, adding distance between me and what is happening, whilst the tingling I feel intensifies.

It is a mist, swirling in the air above the body from which it is manifesting, and around the woman that still sits on the back of my physical form, though it is not touching her. It grows larger, and quickly takes shape, solidifying as it does. I open my mouth to say something, but close it again. What I see is something for which only the word *beast* comes to mind. It has grown to a height of at least six feet, a deep gray that is almost black, vaguely human in shape, with short limbs in the place of arms. But the head, continuing to solidify, is a grotesque parody of the human equivalent. I turn away, not wanting to look any more, an immense fear clenching my phantom bowels. The tingling reaches an all new level and I feel an almighty tug—

Chapter 15

I break from the stupor that has left me lying idle, taking no action against the attacker, her weight crushing me against the ground.

"Get the hell off me you crazy bitch!" I shout, squirming, trying to break free. "I don't know your sister or have any idea what you're talking about. Please." My voice hitches on the last word, showing my fear. Lucas is still crying, so close to me, but I'm able to do nothing to comfort him.

I feel a shifting of her weight, and the knife withdraws from my back and my left arm is freed. The woman stands, and I roll to my side, ready to grab at her, but she has stepped back and is standing out of my reach, looking down at me. In her face I see concern, almost sorrow. "I'm so sorry," she says, "if only you remembered." Then she turns and runs.

"Hey, stop. Get back here." I shakily stand, the pain in my back exploding into white hot fire, a dull ache in my head, mostly from the hit it took against the ground when I was knocked down. I also notice my trousers are wet; my bladder has let go at some point during the ordeal.

I think about chasing her, but Lucas's cries are hysterical, a wailing siren from the pram's confines, and I move to him, ignoring my own pain, feeling blood flowing from my lower back, and the side of my face from the gash in my forehead. The danger to me seems to have fled, and I need to tend to him.

With a hammering heart in my chest, I lean over and right the pram, unstrapping Lucas from his harness. His face is red, and awash with tears, snot bubbling from his nose. I

lift him from the pram, pulling him close and holding him tight. A momentary feeling of pure relief washes over me, but is quickly gone. I breathe in his innocent baby smell as I rock him gently to calm his crying. With each rock I feel the knife is plunging back into my back over and over, the pain causing tears to fall. I am confused as to what has just happened, but the relief is far greater. There will be time to wonder about this woman, and what she was doing, but that's for later.

"Shhh little one. Daddy's got you. We're going to be okay." I continue to rock him, trying as best I can to ignore the pain it causes my body, for his crying is a pain in the soul, something that transcends any physical ache to my flesh. I keep an eye in the direction the attacker ran, making sure she doesn't come back, and not really sure what I'll do if she does.

In time Lucas calms down, his crying becoming hitching sobs that soon abate. My heart too, has returned to an almost normal rhythm. Keeping him against my chest with one arm, for I don't want to let him go, I reach out with my other to grab the pram. With the cool wind blowing at my back, and the wetness of blood seeping from the wound, I head for home.

Epilogue

Three days after Nigel was returned to his wounded body, a heavyset lady stands outside his house, a smile on her face, long dark hair fluttering around her head from a cool wind. It is in the late hours of the night, darkness enshrouding both the house and lady watching it.

She cocks her head as though listening to someone speak, nodding her head. She turns to face a man she knows is standing beside her, though he cannot be seen by her or anyone else. A man who, even though it is winter, is standing outside in a pair of striped pyjamas. Even though not seen, his words reach her mind clearly.

"I cannot help but feel guilty every time," he says to her, knowing she hears his words, though not through her ears. "But I need to mislead them so that when the time comes they are surprised and less likely to give something away. Doing so could ruin their salvation." He shakes his head, and continues, "If I could be present and give them a sign, but the *other* would detect my presence and it will all be for nothing." He is silent for a moment.

Eventually the man speaks again. "If he had taken another path to the park, then what would have happened? His boy's life may not have been saved and I would have failed him."

There is a brief pause before she replies, heedless of anyone that may see or hear her words. She has long ago forgone the concern of others' opinions of her seemingly one-sided conversations. "Of course you feel guilt. But the moment of fear when they think something may have gone wrong lasts a brief moment and then they know nothing

more once they are returned. There will always be some that we are not able to help...cherish those we can.

"That path is the way he left you the night you met, so it makes sense it's the way he would return. So it was the perfect place for me to wait; you planned it well. And if he had not shown, well, we had a second plan, and that would have worked." She smiles in the direction of his presence. "Be proud of what you do. I am."

She turns away, and he nods his head, even though no one can see it. "Not only do you save me from total isolation from the world I was once a part of, we work together to save lives."

He pauses for a long time, staring at the house, and sights that exist in another time and place. Eventually, "I don't know how long I can do this. I have longevity on my side, but still..." His words trail off, and are seemingly carried away on the night's frigid air.

They remain watching the house until the horizon begins to glow from the rising sun. With the wind still whipping about her face, the lady turns and walks away. The man follows shortly after; if he could be seen, people would wonder at what weight this man carries on his shoulders, for his posture indicates it is a heavy burden indeed.

Afterword

SHADES OF REALITY is the first piece of fiction I've read by Leigh Haig...but it's enough!

Of course I was aware of the very fine copywriting that he was doing for Bad Moon Books and others in the small press. I had even communicated with him several times by e-mail. He sounded literate, aware of what was going on in dark fiction, and of course it didn't hurt his credibility that he liked several pieces of my work (and I must say he was a perceptive reader, knowing *why* he enjoyed something, understanding what the writer had in mind). Nevertheless, I would guess there are a number of folks with these same credentials who have never written a piece of fiction that is excellent, especially an apparently relative early effort. But that is the case with Leigh's most excellent SHADES OF REALITY.

First, the tale deals with a fear that isn't often written about in dark fiction. One, I don't think, Stephen King has lectured about, when he lists the childhood fears/common adult fears that he exploits in his work. Obviously, he knows of what he speaks, as his work resonates with all of us in the field. But Leigh deals with something else, and since he is a fairly new father, I suspect it is a fear/dread that is very prominent in his mind. A fear that *every* parent harbors: **The fear or dread of losing a child.** This fear is shaped differently as the specific child (children) mature. I venture to guess that SIDS is uppermost in new parents' minds—how many of us have made repeated unnecessary trips into the nursery and checked the crib...only to find the baby still breathing, even snoring gently. Later, I personally lost sleep until both kids were water safe. The fear of losing a youngster to drowning is undoubtedly a very realistic fear, nothing phobic about it at all. The list goes on and on. And Leigh plays on parental fear of losing a child throughout this tale.

Also, he defies the quick fix we see nowadays in so much TV, movies, and books—lack of real plot development. Leigh takes his time, painstakingly developing the rationale behind The Bastard—the monster in the tale—laying out the real problems and even keeping the reader on the edge of his reading chair until almost the last line. In this regard, I'm guessing that Leigh is familiar with some of our predecessors, especially some of the Brit and Irish masters. Long, slow, almost casual development. But I think in this regard his work reminds me of a more modern master, Ted Klein (if you don't know the name, pick up something, novellas, or his novel, THE CEREMONIES—my favorite horror novel). Just the right amount of development, nothing wasted. Mood, tone, and rationale set perfectly.

Even though the story development is slow and meticulous, I would add that the plot is extremely compelling, keeping the reader hooked while events unfold. As any writer knows, this is not easy, to spend the time/pages necessary to set everything up properly, at the same time keeping the story moving along.

What about this **monster**? Well, I think this Bastard is pretty original, perhaps not quite unique, but obviously we are not dealing with your garden variety possession, vampire, werewolf, or ghost here. Oh, no, what this monster is doing/will do is scaring each and every reader, absolutely chilling all us parents. What to do? What can be done? A true dilemma. With some help, our father addresses both these questions and the dilemma to a very satisfactory conclusion, for sure.

An important aspect of any story is what is going on here beside the surface events? Often this has something to do with what the protagonist has learned. If given a second chance—like our protag here—how is his behavior changed? No question our hero here has learned and changed. But the very best fiction makes the reader think...perhaps even change, if only slightly. Do you suppose any parent reading this doesn't hitch up their pants and pledge to be a better, more watchful parent?

I think the significant question asked about a new writer is: *Is he someone to watch?* Or maybe: *Would I recommend this work to my writer friends?* Or perhaps most important: *Am I going to watch for his byline?* Of course I'd answer a hearty **yes** to all three questions. But in my case, there is a slight tick in my sensibility that by seriously addressing those questions, perhaps—just perhaps—I might be slightly pretentious and presumptuous.

Maybe, if I'm absolutely honest and fair to a fault, I should be asking Leigh: <u>Are you watching for my byline</u>? (Because it is always gratifying when another writer you admire seeks out your work, enjoys it, and makes a positive comment.)

So it goes.

Gene O'Neill—author of
RUSTING CHICKENS and DOUBLEJACK

Authors Note

I don't know about you, but I've always held a fascination in knowing what went on behind the scenes in the creation of a story. So I thought I'd share a little about the tale you've just read; where the genesis of the idea came from, and how it evolved.

But firstly, I want to once again thank you for having the faith in Tom and Billie's choices of fiction, and giving this story a go. I know some will have bought it based purely on the trust of Tom and Billie's choice of fiction, others for the inclusion of words from Mike and Gene; either way, it means a lot.

I'm going to try and keep this spoiler free, but I recommend not reading any further until after you've read the book. How do I know you may be tempted to read this first? Well, I'm a reader, and have found myself often times sneaking a peek at what the author has written at the end. It's kind of like shaking that present before it's time to open it, and get a general idea as to what may be inside. So I certainly cannot fault anyone for doing likewise.

I've got a daughter who, at the time I started writing this, was around 18 months (she's now well past five). She had had sleeping problems in her early months, so it was not uncommon for either myself or my wife (or even both, on those really bad nights) having had to get up to her during the night...quite often multiple times. On one such night, I had returned to bed and read the clock as being earlier than it showed when I had first pried the eyes open upon hearing the crying from the room next door. I recall a momentary bafflement at that, before putting it down to nothing more than puffy, sleep riddled eyes misreading the clock. But it stuck with me, kind of a *what-if* situation, and what events could lead to such a thing occurring.

Enter Michael McBride. I hope all readers of this book are aware of this man and his writing talent (as to those of Gene O'Neill, a lovely man who was too kind in offering to be involved in this book, with the contribution of the afterword). I've known Mike for a good number of years and I think he knew there was a part of me that wanted to write but for which I always had excuses for it not happening. It was not uncommon for Mike to ask, via e-mail, if I was writing anything, and offer a lot of positive encouragement. After my *Christmas Breakdown* sale (in the 2009 Festive Fear anthology from Tasmaniac Press), well, Mike amped up the pressure and indicated I should use the momentum and write some more, try my hand at a longer piece. I wanted to, but was stumped as to what I should write (I am not one with a great imagination). Then to the surface of my memories rose that recalled night where I had read the clock wrong. I toyed with that, and tried to think what it could mean, and where would it lead. In about September of 2009, I started writing.

Having not done a lot of writing before this, I had no technique, and I admit, no clue. So I started by writing the seed of the story, but I still didn't know at that time what it would mean, until the return to the bed revealed the protagonist *still* being asleep, yet standing right there. Enter the niggles I had during the pregnancy with our daughter, the fears of a first time parent, and the story evolved to what it ended up becoming. I have vivid memories of the nights when our girl slept through, those rare, glorious nights, which were tinged with fear when we'd wake in the morning, having not heard from her; the spike of fear that something had happened to her, the only possible reason she didn't wake and cry out in the dark hours of night. Enter the element of cot death into the story. The rest pretty much came together as I wrote. There was no plan, no roadmap I was following. I just sat down of an evening after she had been put to bed, and typed away, letting the story take the path it did.

While I am sure the writing reflects someone with little writing experience, I was very pleased with the general theme of the tale, and how it came together. As the ending drew close, I had no idea what was coming but was a little surprised that it ended the way it did. I love the novel Cujo, and King showing balls to end it with the death of an innocent child (that, alas, Hollywood was not able to follow through with). I have always felt there are not enough books out there that take the route of a heart-wrenching conclusion. With that in mind, am I disappointed in my ending? Not at all: that just happens to be the way the tale finished.